The Space Marine's Stolen Bride

I0562154

Taylor Neptune

ISBN: 978-1634810500

CONTENTS

Threat

Donnchadh

Donnchadh's head was in his hands as his mind raced. As a trained warrior, he never panicked, but the threat in the satellite mail that he'd just read was coming close to pushing him into a panic attack.

Mr. Cross had found him. Donnchadh hadn't been able to enlist with Kandalph Space Marines, Inc. under an assumed name; KSM had some of the best technological resources in the known universe, and they'd have found out if he had tried to deceive them. Since they had money, power, and military might, it was never a good idea to cross them or try to commit fraud. The cost of hiring a paper-smith to cover his trail would've exceeded the money that he hoped to make inside of KSM, so he'd been upfront. And look where that had gotten him: right in Mr. Cross's crosshairs.

Donnchadh leaned back in his chair. He was going to die. His little sister, young Saoirse, was going to die. Gairbith, his worthless brother, had absolutely ruined the entire family. Gairbith had a chronic gambling addiction and had amassed an enormous debt that had already resulted in their father's death. The amount was too big for anybody to pay off. Donnchadh wasn't going to be able to stop them from murdering his entire family.

Donnchadh had tried his best. He'd negotiated an extension on the repayment, accepting their usurious interest rate of 30% per month while he tried to scrounge together enough money. But the end of the repayment period had passed, and they were now even deeper into debt.

Donnchadh and Saoirse hadn't heard from Gairbith for two months; Donnchadh had finding skills, but so did Gairbith. He knew what to do when he wanted to drop off the face of the planet, so Donnchadh couldn't sense him. He was gone, leaving his brother and sister to face Mr. Cross and his band of thugs.

It should have worked out. Donnchadh had signed up with KSM so that he'd be able to pay down the debt; KSM only took the best, but they paid accordingly. But he'd been signed up for a contract to bring fertile females to Dalat, only to be bumped off of the team at the last minute. The Yuenanren had decided that they didn't need as many women as they'd first wanted, so the KSM team was reduced accordingly. As the most junior member of the team, Donnchadh had been sent back to the base to sit on his heels and wait for another contract.

Unlike Gairbith, Donnchadh couldn't just up and go. For one thing, KSM employees didn't disappear. For another, he had Saoirse to think about, especially since they were now orphans due to the death of their father. Their mother had died when Saoirse was born, meaning Donnchadh had raised her almost by himself, learning how to change diapers and prepare bottles, taking Saoirse to the healer for her checkups, singing her to sleep when she woke up in the middle of the night, and more. Saoirse, though she was Donnchadh's sister, had been raised almost as his child. As a warrior, their father had had zero interest in caring for Saoirse when she was a baby. Of course, he'd paid for everything, but Donnchadh sometimes wished that he'd had a little more help from the rest of his family.

Donnchadh's stomach growled. He might as well go to the

commissary on the base. While he didn't have a contract, he wasn't paid anything. He was expected to go through training, and while he was on the bench, he'd have food and lodging. But sitting around on the KSM base didn't really help pay down Gairbith's debt.

Donnchadh put on his uniform and was almost out the door when his glow pad buzzed. He sighed and turned towards it, then he ran to it when he saw that the screen said that Saoirse was calling.

Saoirse

Donnchadh

"Donn!"

"Saoirse," he replied with a little less enthusiasm. "What's up with you?"

"You'll never guess what just happened."

Saoirse was ten years younger than Donnchadh, but sometimes it felt as if he were 100 years older than she was. He cut to the chase.

"What?"

"Guess!"

"No."

He could practically see Saoirse pouting. It had worked when he was younger and terrified of making a mistake with her, so she'd kept the habit. She also frequently got her way when she used tears.

"I got accepted into the healer's hall!"

Donnchadh rubbed his forehead.

"That's great news."

It wasn't. Healers were well-respected on Releon, but they were highly compensated, which meant that her tuition would cost an absolute fortune.

Stars above, how could Gairbith have beggared their family? Maybe before Gairbith landed them in an unmanageable amount of debt, they could have scraped together enough money if all three of them worked.

Now, it was impossible.

"I'm so proud of you," he told Saoirse. He was. He wasn't going to tell her now, right when she was so elated, that there was no chance that she'd be able to finish her training even if she started. They didn't have the money, and Mr. Cross would soon kill both of them, since Gairbith had vanished.

She kept talking about her potential specialties, but Donnchadh stopped listening to her. He should probably bring her inside of the KSM base, but how? KSM had the tightest security possible — so tight that he doubted he'd be able to get clearance to get her inside. They allowed wives to live inside of the base, but those were the only females around. Could he pretend that Saoirse, his eighteen-year-old sister, was his wife? No, they'd find out.

He interrupted Saoirse mid-sentence. "I've got to go. I'm starving, and the commissary is closing in another 20 minutes."

"Oh," he heard her say. Her sad tone made him almost relent, but his stomach was starting to get hungrier and hungrier as he waited out here. Training used a lot of energy. "That's okay."

"I'll talk to you later, a leanbh," he told Saoirse.

"Later," she said. The glow pad went dark.

He sighed. He had to figure out a way to protect her, and it was probably going to crush her dreams. He'd have to find out if the healers would let her postpone her training. Probably not. The healers were strict about whom they permitted into their ranks, and Saoirse would probably have this one shot.

He had a lump in his throat. He was the problem solver in the family. His dad had provided the money, but Donnchadh had run the household, fixing the problems of the family members. Gairbith had finally gotten into trouble that Donnchadh couldn't fix with hard work, something to which Gairbith was allergic. He ran in the fast lane, chasing credits and beautiful women while Donnchadh kept his feet firmly planted on the ground. Something had to give. Donnchadh had done everything that he could, and it still wasn't enough. As long as he had breath in his body, though, he'd fight to protect Saoirse and himself from Gairbith's mistakes.

He finally got out of the door with a few minutes to spare, heading towards the commissary right as they were packing everything up.

Sparring

Donnchadh

He accepted a bowl of simple soup with cabbage and beef, reminding him of home and the food that his mother had cooked before her death. KSM didn't skimp when it came to provisioning their men, and they always ate well. They had some of the best chefs in the universe at their bases.

He finally finished his food and

put his bowl on the turning rack at the edge of the room. Right as he left the commissary, he ran into his roommate, Giang, who was one of the Yuenanren. As part of the agreement with the government of Dalat, some of the young warriors on Dalat had to sign up for KSM. There'd been an abundance of applications for the spots, especially since their training was taking place in the base on Dalat, and many of the newest members of Donnchadh's regiment were Yuenanren.

The way that the Yuenanren trained was nothing like what Donnchadh had seen before on Releon, but he had to say that their style of fighting was pretty effective. Donnchadh was bigger than Giang, but Giang made up for the height difference with his speed. He loved testing himself against Giang; their fighting styles were so different that there was about a 50% chance of winning each match.

"Hi, Giang."

Giang nodded hello. "Do you

want to spar?"

"Yeah." It was as if Giang could read his mind. There was nothing he wanted more than to lose himself in fighting; he needed to stop thinking about Mr. Cross murdering his sister or worse.

They headed to the base's sparring room. It was nearly empty at this hour, most of the space marines resting in their rooms before they got up for tomorrow's training.

The only person in the room was Horus, who was making the biggest punching bag, which weighed more than 800 libra, swing hard back and forth, pulling on the chain almost enough to pull the bag from its mount on the ceiling. He was a guy from Aigyptos, and one of the biggest guys on the base. There were some rumors that he used drugs for his physique; looking at his arm muscles, Donnchadh believed the rumors. They were bigger than his head.

Donnchadh and Giang went to the side to grab big staves. Giang began to warm up by spinning his staff in his hand.

"Care to spar?" Horus had a thick accent in Standard, but his meaning was clear. His invitation was nothing like Giang's friendly one. Giang only meant for them to get some exercise. Horus obviously wanted to establish dominance over Donnchadh; he knew that he'd be hearing about any defeat for the rest of his time with KSM, which at minimum would be five years.

Donnchadh turned to look at him and sized up the competition.

Donnchadh might not be as fast as Giang, but he probably had enough speed to challenge this meathead.

"Yeah."

Horus came to the side to unwrap his wrists and pick up his own staff. He chose the longest one, the one that they kept on the end. It was only for the largest men, because it was overwhelmingly enormous. Giang was about 7 feet tall, and the staff was longer than that by a few feet. Horus spun it and then tossed it up in the air, swiping the staff in front of himself.

"Don't hurt yourself," Giang cautioned as he ducked under Horus' swing. "That's a big staff."

"I can handle it, short stuff. That's why I don't spar with losers like you. It's not worth the time."

Anger burned in Donnchadh's gut. Giang was shorter than some of the other KSM men, but he was just as fierce of a fighter as the rest of them, and he wasn't the shortest man at the base.

"Let's go," Donnchadh told

Horus, stepping back.

They stepped into the clear space. The mostly bare sparring room was made exactly for fights like this. The punching bags were in one section, and there were mats made for sparring. They had rubber so that it would grip their feet and cushion any falls. Donnchadh and Horus should be wearing some padding and helmets, but neither of them had any protective gear on.

Was it reckless? Maybe. But Donnchadh was going to teach Horus a lesson that he wouldn't forget.

They moved in a circle on their sparring mat, neither one willing to attack first. Then Donnchadh watched Horus step forward and bring his staff down, trying to crush Donnchadh with all of his weight and strength. Instead of trying to fight it, Donnchadh slid to the side, making Horus overbalance and fall forward. He followed with a quick leg sweep to make Horus' legs come out from under him. Then Donnchadh fell onto Horus' back, hard, and he heard the grunt that meant that he'd knocked the breath out of him.

Good.

Horus slapped the mat. Donnchadh got off of him, though he kept his staff in his hand. He didn't trust Horus to take his defeat gracefully.

Horus' face was red. "Who knew that Releons fought dirty?"

Giang snorted. "He beat you fairly."

"Whatever, short stuff," Horus sneered, sweeping some of his black hair back from his forehead. "Neither of you are good enough to take me in a fair fight. I'm wasting my time here." He got his wrist wraps and left the sparring room quickly.

"Do you still want to spar with me?" Giang asked Donnchadh.

"I think that I've lost the taste for it at the moment," he said, looking at the staff that Horus hadn't bothered to put back on the rack. "Let's just go back to our room."

Giang nodded, putting his staff away. He grunted a little when he picked up Horus' staff, but he was able to maneuver it into the right spot.

Together, they walked through the nearly empty hallways to get a little rest.

Test Run

Donnchadh

The next afternoon, Donnchadh was totally out of breath. In this simulation, he needed to find a target item listed on the mock manifest. It was a small box, and he had to evade the KSM men who were tasked with preventing his team from obtaining their objective.

All of them were equipped with laser guns. They got points for each hit, and there were certain spots on the body which immediately deactivated them and forced them to leave the field. Half of Donnchadh's team was down, but he was close to the box.

He could find things if he'd touched them before. At the very beginning of the simulation, he'd made sure to handle it before the clock started, ignoring the side eye from the other team. KSM didn't look for lost items often, but Donnchadh used his skills all the same. He wasn't the kind of man to half-do anything.

It was a level playing field. Many of the space marines had some extra skills of some sort. Giang had a little precognition, which, now that Donnchadh thought about it, explained how Giang was so fantastic as a fighter. Donnchadh was doubly proud of himself for beating him.

Giang was at Donnchadh's back as they entered the building where the box was held. Giang moved silently towards the room where it was held. They turned on their x-vision goggles, showing them the room beyond. One of the marines on the opposing team was in the room.

"Diversion," Giang whispered to Donnchadh. He pulled a grenade out of his pack.

Giang had decided to carry a smoke grenade in here. That was a smart move. Donnchadh watched as Giang pulled out the pin, then the two of them went running outside of the building.

There was a cry of fear as

whoever was inside of that room saw the smoke grenade coming towards them. They watched as the form of a marine ran outside. Their laser guns were ready, and they hit the core target, one of the ones that would shut him down entirely. The uniform glowed red as it drew him towards the sideline.

Giang and Donnchadh ran past the deactivated opponent. As they got closer, Donnchadh realized that it was Horus. Horus glared at them, but he couldn't fight the force of his uniform as it pulled him to the side.

Donnchadh ran into the building and headed straight for the box, the smoke making his eyes sting. He realized that he should've put something over his nose and mouth, but it was too late now. He had the box in his hand and pressed the button that ended the simulation.

Bells rang as soon as Donnchadh completed his mission, ending everything. He and Giang brought the small box to the meeting point.

"Well done," their drill sergeant

said to Donnchadh. "I think that's the fastest simulation I've ever seen."

Horus was glaring at Donnchadh, but he brushed it off. He wasn't here for a pissing contest. All of this was part of his job.

"Thank you, sir." He was glad that he'd been praised; he'd be doing this sort of thing for the next five years at least. If he allowed himself to focus on what was going wrong, though, he'd mess up and end up with demerits.

Besides, the money that he'd

earn might be enough to get protection for his sister or somehow put her through her healer's training. Gairbith was gone, long gone, apparently missing the sense of duty and honor that their father had drilled into Donnchadh in the cradle.

"That's it for today, gentlemen," the sergeant shouted. "Back here at 08:00 tomorrow morning."

"Sir, yes, sir," they all chanted.

"Dismissed."

They all went to get changed into everyday clothes. After training sims, especially when they got out early, the men would go to the base's nearby bar. When the alcohol was free, it was easy to get drunk and forget all about their duties until the next day.

Donnchadh wasn't a big drinker normally, but he also knew that he'd be the odd man out if he never went to drink with them. So he followed the men to drink some ruou, the strong local brew which was made out of rice distilled several times, not unlike vodka. When they got to the bar, Donnchadh chose a seat in the corner where he could be quiet and not be forced to match the other guys glass for glass, shot for shot.

He stared straight forward as the other guys rehashed the simulation that they'd just been through. The teams changed every time, so the camaraderie inside of his regiment was always tight, even when they were on opposite sides. The ruou couldn't erase the worries that had started with Mr. Cross's mail; Saoirse's good news was anything but good. He was in a tight corner from which he couldn't see his way out.

"A credit for your thoughts?"

Donnchadh blinked before turning to the voice.

"Sir," he said, saluting his superior.

"Why have you put yourself into the corner in the loner's section, private?"

"I'm worn out from today's simulations, sir. Just needed a few minutes of quiet."

Grinning, Commander Stark

said, "I remember my own days of stealing a little time away. It's not easy to adjust to sharing rooms here, not if you've grown up with your own room." Reaching forward to pat Donnchadh's back, he said, "I'm sure that you will soon claim a post that might allow you to pay for your own quarters on the base. I'm certain of it. You have a good night now, private."

Then Commander Stark was gone, going to the bar to order a drink. While he waited, he went to the karaoke machine. He pulled up the list of songs. Was Donnchadh going to have to listen to his commander sing?

Scrambling to his feet, Donnchadh said, "Bye," to his regiment before heading out of the door. He thought about Commander Stark's words as he walked back to his room. Could he make it out of his current dilemma and earn the success that Commander Stark somehow believed that he'd get?

Called by the Warlord

Donnchadh

The next afternoon, Donnchadh wasn't permitted to finish the day's simulation. Commander Stark appeared and pulled him out of training.

"You know what we were talking about yesterday, son?"

"Yes, sir."

"You're about to meet the man who'll put rocket boosters on your career."

Donnchadh breathed slowly, trying to appear cool. He had to admit that he was in a tight corner, though. If the stranger could somehow make Mr. Cross go away or put Donnchadh in a better position, he'd be all ears.

Commander Stark brought Donnchadh into his private chambers, right to the door of his small office. He was entitled to a bigger one, but he insisted on staying in the same office that he'd been given when he was first made an officer. He always said that it helped him connect to the lower-ranking officers.

"What is spoken about here will never be discussed anywhere else, do you understand?"

"Yes, sir."

"Good." Commander Stark tapped the side of his nose. "That attitude will get you far inside of KSM. I'll leave you alone." He turned and left Donnchadh at his office doors.

With a bit of anxiety in his

stomach, Donnchadh walked inside of Commander Stark's office.

Inside was a man who had his back to him, one of the Yuenanren. He was tall, very tall for a Yuenanren, in fact. Giang, who was 7 feet tall, was somewhat above average for the Yuenanren. The man inside was close to Donnchadh's height, if not taller. He was wearing a cloak that had warrior stripes on it. Donnchadh wasn't all that familiar with Dalat's military structure, but he knew that one stripe meant the equivalent of private in the Yuenanren's military structure, and this man had too many stripes to count.

"Hello, Donnchadh."

Donnchadh saluted. "Hello, sir!"

"Won't you take a seat?"

"Yes, sir." Donnchadh sat in one of the luxurious leather seats in front of Commander Stark's desk. He had the uncomfortable feeling that he was sitting on true leather, not the kind that was grown in laboratories. How had Commander Stark gotten real leather?

"Let me introduce myself. I'm Ngo Xuong Xi."

Donnchadh swallowed hard. Ngo Xuong Xi was legendary. He was the one who had negotiated the arrangement for KSM to bring Brides to Dalat, and he'd had the pull to authorize their base here, the base in which Donnchadh was now living. He had been something of a space pirate in his younger days, terrorizing spaceships in the vicinity. When he'd gotten older, he'd retired from piracy and settled into the government, slowly rising to the top and murdering everyone who opposed him. Outside of Dalat, he wasn't as well known; to the outside world and the Intergalactic Federation, Dalat was a democracy. But they were on-planet, and Donnchadh's roommate had told him a little about the current political climate, which was tightly controlled by Ngo Xuong Xi.

"I've heard of you, sir," Donnchadh replied. Huge understatement.

Ngo Xuong Xi looked at

Donnchadh intently, his eyes resting on the muscles that Donnchadh had developed when he thought that he'd become one of Releon's famous feallmharfóir instead of a marine inside of KSM. Space marines had to be strong, yes, but they didn't need to be able to decapitate a male in a single blow and then fade into the shadows.

Donnchadh fought the urge to squirm under Ngo Xuong Xi's gaze. It felt as if he could see right through Donnchadh, see his sister, his brother, and the debt that threatened to swallow him. Donnchadh hadn't had anybody scrutinize him this closely since he applied for KSM.

"I've seen your test records."

"Test records, sir?"

"You're one of the fastest trainees that KSM has ever seen."

Donnchadh didn't know that. The test results were confidential and secret. There were no public rankings.

"Thank you, sir."

"You can fly a spaceship with

expert ease," Ngo Xuong Xi
commented.

"I can, sir. My father owned a
ship, sir, and he taught me how to
use the controls when I was big
enough to reach them, sir."

"I see." Ngo Xuong Xi drummed
his fingers on the desktop.

"I've also heard that you have
some skills related to finding."

"Yes, sir. I can find anything that
I've touched, sir."

"Well, I have a question for you."

"Yes, sir?"

"How would you like to make a little money using those skills for a very important task?"

Donnchadh's heart thumped in his chest. Could Ngo Xuong Xi be offering enough money to clear out Gairbith's gambling debts and send Saoirse through training?

"I'd love to, sir. I would certainly appreciate an opportunity to make a little money."

The warlord leaned back in his chair and smiled widely, his grin nearly going ear to ear. Donnchadh was suddenly just a little worried about what he'd gotten himself into.

"I'm glad to hear it. The details will be sent to you over a secure, encoded line. Your decryption tests show that you can decrypt encrypted code within minutes."

"Yes, sir, that's true." Donnchadh had spent way too many hours in his youth learning about cryptography, which somehow had helped him when he grew up. He was good with computers, very good, and it all started with understanding how they worked and what they could do.

"I'll arrange for a deposit to be sent to your credit account. You'll get the details soon. Dismissed, private."

"Sir, yes, sir." Donnchadh saluted and got to his feet. He hesitated for a moment before bowing to Ngo Xuong Xi, deferring to Yuenanren customs.

With an amused smile lurking at the corners of his mouth, Ngo Xuong Xi inclined his head a fraction of a centimeter.

Donnchadh walked back to his

room in a daze. Could this be the answer to his prayers?

He couldn't deny that there was something about Ngo Xuong Xi that made the hairs on the back of his neck stand up...maybe because he was so dangerous. He'd killed more people than Donnchadh had even met. He thought about asking Giang for more stories about Ngo Xuong Xi, but he decided against it. He got the impression from Commander Stark that this contract was under the table; it was best to keep everything to himself.

Encrypted Message

Donnchadh

When he got back to his room, his glow pad buzzed with a message. A puzzle appeared on his glow pad in a sequence of shapes. Donnchadh realized that Ngo Xuong Xi had been ready for him to say yes; the first test was right here. He didn't want to fail, not with Saoirse's training and Gairbith's debt on the line.

He got out his tablet to trace the

shapes before understanding the sequence. He sketched the next image onto his glow pad.

He watched as the glow pad began to show the details of his assignment. He was being told to hack into KSM's assignment files so that he'd be the transporter for an Oxitan princess who was scheduled to marry Ngo Xuong Xi.

Something sat wrong in Donnchadh's gut, but he couldn't afford to be choosy. The job might be the tiniest bit unethical, but he needed to go through with it.

He'd gone through prober training during his first week, though it was a position reserved for officers of higher rank in the field. Since KSM often dealt with extractions, they trained every one of their space marines in the art of probing. All of them had nano-bots put into their bloodstreams on the first day, and they spent their first week using pleasure-bots to practice their bedroom skills so that they could induce the female orgasm that sent the nano-bots back into their bodies.

If a space marine couldn't pass the

tests by the end of the first week, he'd

be sent home, his five-year contract

null. Not all of them were probers,

but it certainly helped to have a lot of

them on hand. KSM could hire extra

mercenaries as back-up, but probing

was something that was only done by

them with their proprietary nano-

bots.

He took his tablet and connected

to the network that only the officers

at the major rank and above could

access. He'd figured out the password
on the first day. Who would think
that "marine" was a secure
password?

His heart thumping, slightly
afraid that KSM's cybersecurity
would be stronger than the Releon
computers that he'd hacked, he
found the files related to
assignments.

He frowned as he opened his file.
He'd been assigned to transport
Princess Celeste, who was slated to
marry Ngo Xuong Xi. Why was it

already done?

He realized that Commander Stark must know what was going on. He'd arranged the whole thing. This first task had been the second test. He needed to tell them that he was already assigned after he successfully accessed the files.

He touched his glow pad to write "Done."

It faded as he wrote it. He waited for a second before his glow pad said, "Connection Terminated."

Donnchadh sat back down on his

bed and rubbed his face with his

hands. What was going on?

Assignment

Donnchadh

The next morning, Donnchadh was called to the KSM Assignment Office right after breakfast.

"Hello, private," his CO said.

"Sir," Donnchadh said, saluting.

"We've got a contract for you."

Donnchadh tried to look surprised.

"A contract, sir?"

"Yes, one of our transport

contracts." His CO, Sergeant Park, tapped a few things to bring a hologram to life.

Donnchadh felt like he got the wind knocked out of him when he saw the woman in the hologram.

"Pretty, isn't she?"

Donnchadh just nodded.

"This lady is Princess Celeste of Elysia on Oxitan. She's slated to marry Ngo Xuong Xi, the current president of Dalat. Are you ready for your first assignment?"

President? More like dictator. But

Donnchadh held his tongue, trying
not to tip his hand.

"Yes, sir."

"Good. We'll provision your ship.
We're going to put you on an initial
test run with two of your regiment
members. We've seen you in action in
your simulations, but it's time for you
to use a real spaceship."

"Yes, sir."

"I have your instruction card and
access pass. You'll meet a team at the
docks for pick-up this afternoon.
Pack and be ready by 15:00.

Dismissed."

"Yes, sir." Donnchadh took the cards that had appeared in Sergeant Park's hand before saluting and leaving.

Donnchadh had nothing to do for the rest of the morning except pack, which he could do in 5 minutes. He went to the commissary to eat lunch, glad to get there before the rest of the space marines. If he was too late because a simulation ran a little too long, he could be faced with eating rabbit food, just fresh vegetables native to Dalat, depending on what they had that day. If he wanted something with protein in it — which he always did — he needed to show up earlier. The prospect of meat for meals was a key factor in just how fast Donnchadh's team finished simulations. Nobody wanted to go hungry. Sure, KSM would always provide enough to fill their stomachs, but Donnchadh was strangely empty and still mentally hungry even if he'd eaten an enormous amount of vegetables.

He ate alone in the commissary, since nearly all of the marines on the base were in simulations at the moment. He was alone with his thoughts. He had heard around the base that KSM's Brides usually didn't know what they were getting into. KSM ensured that their future mates were disease-free and capable of providing for them. In addition, KSM had technology that could slice them up and spit them out in perfect form so that they'd conform to their future mate's ideals. Donnchadh had learned about the surgery when he'd been trained to release his nano-bots intra-vaginally; once the female orgasmed, the nano-bots would return and tell him what was wrong and automatically configure the surgeon-bot to adjust whatever needed to be fixed. It was nothing that hurt, since they were anesthetized, but he wasn't sure how he felt about all of it. Saoirse, his little sister, was 18, after all. KSM could take her if they wanted to.

Was that the answer to running

from Mr. Cross? He doubted that he'd be attacked while he was part of KSM, but maybe he should encourage Saoirse to sign up as a Bride. She was willful and independent, yes, but she had a good sense of self-preservation, too. She didn't know about Gairbith's debts; he hadn't told her yet, wanting to shield her from reality. But the day would come soon that she'd need to know what was going on.

He sighed. He didn't want his sister to become a Bride, a

commodity. KSM guaranteed the beauty and fertility of each Bride, and he hated the thought of one of his marine brothers probing her. The only time when they didn't probe a Bride was when the recipient requested that his Bride be untouched. They didn't perform any surgery at all, then.

He needed to know more about the job that he'd do after the test run, so he put his tray away on the spinning rack before going back to his room. When he got there, he saw a simple calling card on his desk. It was engraved with the symbol that he'd written on his glow pad yesterday, so he knew that it was from Ngo Xuong Xi. He put it into his pocket for safekeeping.

Getting his tablet out of his desk, he pulled up the file for his assignment. Seeing her picture in two dimensions made the impact of her beauty hit him a little less hard. She was stunning, true, but not as breathtaking as earlier. He saw that Ngo Xuong Xi had requested that

Princess Celeste be untouched. There was a marker that said that she was still a virgin. It was hard to believe when she was so beautiful, but KSM was very thorough when it came to researching future Brides, especially ones intended for major power players. KSM wasn't in the business of delivering defective Brides.

Test Run

Donnchadh

Later that afternoon, Donnchadh made his way to the docks before the scheduled 15:00 departure. He was the first one there. There were three glasses of nutri-drink, vile green stuff that could boost his immune system to repel almost every alien ailment. He pinched his nose as he drank one glass of the stuff, but he couldn't get rid of the bitter aftertaste.

He sat down at one of the levitating chairs in front of the control panel. As he sat, he felt the small bulge in his pocket where Ngo Xuong Xi's calling card was. He took it out and looked at it, tracing the engraving with his thumb.

When the entire Intergalactic Federation was connected by open lines, the only people who used calling cards, an anachronism that came from the time before communications had been standardized, were criminals and politicians. Donnchadh honestly didn't see much of a difference between the two.

If Donnchadh could go through with his assignment for Ngo Xuong Xi, then he'd probably get a promotion. Part of him had no desire to tangle with this lovely female and carry her away for the Yuenanren warlord, but he needed to protect Saoirse. In this case, he'd protect her at the expense of Princess Celeste. He'd do anything for his little sister, and he'd see the secret assignment through.

He put the calling card away and started going through the pre-flight checklist. He would try to make the most of today and utilize it as the learning experience that it was intended to be, a gift to prepare him for the transport trip that would enable him to pay off his debt and send his sister through training. Maybe he could get a private room as Commander Stark suggested, though he liked Giang's company.

The door opened. Donnchadh

spun around and got to his feet,
sticking his hand out to greet the
other two marines who were joining
him. One was Oxomese, with tan skin
and stick-straight black hair. He
shook Donnchadh's hand and
slapped him on the back.

"Ready to go?"

The other marine was a little
more retiring. Instead of shaking
Donnchadh's offered hand, he just
gave him a nod.

Donnchadh didn't know either of
them very well, though he'd seen

them in the commissary and during a few simulations, so he asked, "What are your names?"

"Jinar," said the Oxomese one.

"Lothair," said the Oxitan.

"Glad to meet you. I'm Donnchadh."

Pleasantries over, all of them sat in levitating chairs to look at the control panel. Donnchadh had steered a spaceship many times, but he noticed that the Oxomese's hands were shaking a little.

"Don't worry, marine," he told

him. "This is even easier than the sims."

"I hope so," Jinar told him. "I've never flown any spacecraft before."

"Trust me, it's easy."

With that, Donnchadh brought the engines to life. With the roar of the engines behind them, Donnchadh lifted the ship off of the base's launching pad and into the sky.

The force of their departure pushed them back into their seats, covered in gel precisely for this purpose. During take-off, there were straps that would automatically wrap around their bodies like snakes.

Donnchadh leaned all the way back in his chair and waited for the pressure to ease up. The simulations had taught him that he only had to bear it for a few minutes before it was over. He counted his heartbeats.

When he got to 120, the pressure eased. They'd made it out of Dalat's atmosphere and were ready to go to the next planet over.

He swiped his instruction card through the reader on the control panel. Jinar, Lothair, and Donnchadh read the directions for their journey. The instruction card automatically set their course for the planet for which they were heading. It wasn't even a day's journey away at light speed.

"Well, that's it," Lothair said. "I'm going to go to sleep. I'll tell my tablet to wake me up when we're near the drop site."

They'd been through the simulations a dozen times or more. They went to a planet, dropped the pods, and came back. Simple and easy.

"Me, too," Jinar yawned. "I didn't get much sleep last night. My sore shoulders kept me up; I couldn't find a comfortable position."

"It looks like we're all sleeping until we get there," Donnchadh said. "I'll make sure to set the ship to wake us with an alarm if anything needs our attention."

The other two saluted him before heading to their bunks. They had very small capsules on this ship, stacked on top of each other. While there wasn't all that much space, they had privacy inside of a coffin-like enclosure. Donnchadh highly preferred the relatively spacious area that he was granted inside of his shared room, but he'd take what he could get. He needed some shut-eye.

He'd been thinking about the assignment to obtain Princess Celeste all last night. Why had he been chosen for this task?

Drop

Donnchadh

"Approaching Cria."

Donnchadh slid out of his capsule and got to his feet. Jinar and Lothair were soon out of their capsules as well. The three of them headed to the control panel and sat down in their chairs again.

Donnchadh stared in dismay at the terrifyingly gray planet in front of him. He couldn't see the oceans or vegetations due to the clouds that covered everything. He thought about the sedated Brides who were in the ship's hold. Would they be happy on Cria?

"Release them," Lothair said softly. "Then we can go back to sleep."

Jinar took the decision out of Donnchadh's hands by leaning over and pulling the lever that would release the pods. The pods all had guidance systems built into them, but they could manually override one that landed straight on some kind of sharp rock. Generally, the pods tried to find a body of water deep enough to take the impact of landing without damaging the expensive cargo inside.

He wished the new Brides well; they'd be delivered near the men who had funded their extraction and delivery by KSM. Donnchadh felt a pang when he thought about young Saoirse being put inside of one of those pods. No, becoming a Bride was not the solution. He'd never do this to his little sister.

He was rubbing the back of his neck when Jinar said, "Second thoughts, marine?"

He turned to look at him. "Just not used to this, that's all."

"Don't worry about what we're doing," Jinar advised. "On Oxom, all of our marriages are arranged. We know that love-matches are common in the rest of the galaxy, but my parents and grandparents think that it is lunacy. Stars above, young people have no idea what kind of person they want to be with as they grow older. It's better to let older and wiser people choose," he concluded with the total assurance and certitude of someone who had been trained in his beliefs since childhood.

"On Releon, we marry for love." Donnchadh didn't add anything, and Jinar fell silent. He didn't want to start a fight here, not when there were only three of them.

"It's not my place to judge. It's my job."

"Remember that, soldier, the next time that you need to pull the lever."

Lothair got to his feet. "I'm going back to my capsule now." He left Donnchadh and Jinar at the control panel.

"Hey. Nobody in KSM enjoys delivering unconscious Brides to unknown men, but our researchers always make sure that the Brides are well cared for. Every physical ailment is addressed during the surgery, as you know, after they are probed. I'm fine with what we do, even if I don't really enjoy it. We're compensated well enough to make it worth it."

"I'm sure that I'll get used to it."

Jinar grinned, showing his white teeth, which gleamed with a little of the red light from the control panel. "You may not believe it right now, but eventually, you'll get used to it."

Trashed

Donnchadh

When they got back to the base, Donnchadh took his things and headed straight for his room.

He frowned. The door was open, which was strange. Giang had old habits that made him almost compulsively lock the outer door to their room.

He approached his room slowly, getting a stunner out of his bag. If there was someone waiting in there, a thug from Mr. Cross, he'd be ready.

But when he looked through the doorway, all he saw was Giang with a black eye and their furniture in splinters.

"Giang?"

Giang spun to look at Donnchadh. "Oh, you're back. Good."

Donnchadh walked into the room cautiously, sweeping the room with his eyes, but he didn't see anybody besides Giang.

"What happened to you?"

"I don't know how a couple of thugs made it onto the base, but they came into our room while I was sleeping. I wasn't quick enough to dodge a fist to the face which woke me up. They looked for you everywhere in here, and they weren't afraid to tear stuff up. Stars above, what are you involved in? Why did the thugs come here?"

"I'm sorry," Donnchadh said. He wanted to protect Saoirse, and he'd thought that joining KSM would be sufficient protection from Mr. Cross' men. Instead, his roommate had been roughed up. "I'll tell my superiors. They'll probably kick me out when they realize that I have someone after me." Donnchadh rubbed his face with his hand. Saoirse and he wouldn't have another chance.

Giang's face was softening, despite the black eye. "No, it's okay. I haven't reported it yet; it just happened. If you can replace all of our furniture and make the room look like it has never been trashed, we'll just forget that this happened.

I'll say that I got this black eye from sparring. But you're paying for a retina lock on our door."

"Deal."

"Make sure that you buy all the furniture from the base's warehouse. It would generate too many questions if we suddenly had furniture from Dalat."

"I'll take care of it."

He walked to the warehouse and bought furniture that he couldn't afford with most of the credits in his account. He didn't see an alternative;

he needed all the money he could get to pay off Mr. Cross, but if KSM kicked him out because he had a dangerous man after him, all of his prospects to get more credits, the kind of money that he needed to pay the debt, would be gone. He went and chose all that he needed to replace the furniture that had been smashed during the thugs' visit and loaded it on a hover cart before pushing all of it back to his room. He really needed to fulfill this contract now as he was nearly out of money. Saoirse didn't have a job yet, so he provided for her. Without any money, she'd go hungry. He'd never let that happen. Not ever.

He spent most of the afternoon unloading and rearranging their furniture to conceal what had happened. He took the ruined furniture to the incinerator to hide the evidence. He didn't want anybody to know about Mr. Cross and Gairbith's debt. He supposed that Giang might deserve an explanation, but Giang hadn't pushed for one as long as Donnchadh cleaned up the

mess. He sighed. Giang's small
amount of precognition apparently
didn't work when he was asleep.

* * *

A few hours later, when the lights
on the base went out, Giang was
already snoring loudly enough to
make their bunks slightly vibrate
with the sound. Donnchadh got out
of his bunk to go to the glow pad.
He'd already learned that Giang was
a deep sleeper; it was nearly
impossible to get him out of bed
without an alarm that might cause

permanent hearing loss.

He swiped the calling card that had been left for him and held his breath as the glow pad buzzed again and again. Finally, Ngo Xuong Xi picked up on the other end. He was smiling at Donnchadh, a smile that made Donnchadh shiver a little.

"Yes or no?"

Donnchadh's answer would change the course of his life. He could adhere to the principles of honor that his father had drilled into him and expect a message that his little sister was dead all because of Gairbith's gambling debts, or he could choose his duty to his sister and his overwhelming need to keep her safe.

"Yes."

Duty was going to win today. He'd do nearly anything to keep Saoirse safe and happy, even if it made his stomach churn.

Ethics

Donnchadh

The next day, Donnchadh could feel bile rising in his throat as he sat in his ethics class. It was mandatory for all of the KSM employees, including the support staff. As the professor droned on about different philosophical frameworks, Donnchadh stared at his tablet, the words bouncing off of his ears. He couldn't care less about the different types of consequentialism. Was the universe trying to tell him that he'd agreed to do something wrong?

But he was already on the path. He'd confirmed it with Ngo Xuong Xi; he couldn't claim that he didn't know what was going on. He clearly had the information he needed to make the decision. With his back against the wall, he was making the only choice that he could if he wanted to keep Saoirse safe from Mr. Cross's thugs. Besides, he didn't want to make an enemy of Ngo Xuong Xi, especially since he'd be based on Dalat for the foreseeable future.

He should reframe this as a good opportunity. He was lucky that the most powerful man on Dalat had entrusted him with his future wife.

Giang turned his head so that he was looking at Donnchadh. Donnchadh's face turned a little red. He knew that Giang had precognition; how strongly was he triggering it? Could Giang see Donnchadh making a fatal mistake?

Even if he asked Giang what

would happen, there wasn't anything that Donnchadh could do to change his future. He'd signed his deal with the devil, and that was it. He'd committed.

Finally, the professors wrote their assignment on the board. There were a bunch of ethical case studies that they had to read for the next class. Joy. More work that would take up their valuable and rare free time.

Giang and Donnchadh packed up their things. As they walked back to their room, Giang pulled Donnchadh aside in a small hallway, away from the rest of their regiment.

"What are you involved in?"

"It's nothing to worry about."

"You didn't notice when the professor called on you in ethics class. Everyone waited for you to answer, but it was as if you weren't there."

"Some matters are too large to discuss. Sometimes, things have to be handled and left alone." He meant it as a warning, but Giang saw straight through him.

"You're not alone, you know. We haven't known each other for all that long, but we're roommates. At this point, I hope that you consider me a friend. Whatever you're involved in, I don't want to believe that it's so bad that you can't use a friendly ear. Talk to me when you're ready."

Giang neatly spun around Donnchadh, joining the flow of their regiment mates to go back to their quarters. Donnchadh leaned against the hallway wall, staring at the ceiling. Could he risk telling Giang?

No, he decided. Giang was a good man, a great friend even, but he was also one of the Yuenanren. He trusted Giang, but he didn't necessarily trust Giang's family. Having Ngo Xuong Xi's wife would give them political leverage if they wanted it. If Ngo Xuong Xi's Bride was stolen from him in transit, he'd be utterly ruined.

Textbooks

Donnchadh

The next morning, his glow pad buzzed before Giang's alarm went off. He saw Saoirse's name flash, and he quickly accepted the call.

His little sister had bags under her eyes. She was fond of experimenting with cosmetics, something that she'd done just for herself. None of the rest of her family members understood how they worked. She normally kept artistic makeup on her face, but her face was bare now.

"What's wrong, Saoirse?"

She seemed close to the verge of tears. "I tried to buy some of my study materials...my books...and my credit pass was denied."

Donnchadh had no idea that Saoirse would need her school materials so soon.

He watched a tear go down her cheek and drop off of her chin before she asked, "I know that Daddy didn't leave us anything when he died. Are we broke, Donn?"

He didn't want to lie to her. He'd sheltered her for a long time, but he wasn't going to be able to keep up the facade anymore. They were at the end of their rope now. "Yes."

She began to cry in earnest now, sobs wracking her body. Donnchadh turned to look at Giang, but he was still snoring.

"What are we going to do?"

"I'm working on it, Saoirse. Can you get a loan from somebody?"

"I don't have a job," she protested. "We have no money or collateral. How would I get a loan?"

"Scholarships?"

"You know that the scholarships for healer's training are only for the truly poor, the absolutely destitute."

"Saoirse, you're going to qualify for a scholarship."

She gasped and then began crying harder. "Are you serious?"

"Deadly serious, little sister."

"How did things get so bad?"

He might as well tell her all of it.

"Gairbith is in a huge amount of debt. Dad's death wasn't an accident, even though they made it look like one."

"What are you talking about? What does Gairbith have to do with it? We haven't seen him for months."

"I know."

"How much debt?"

He told her, and she began hyperventilating.

"That's enough money to keep us afloat for 20 years. How could he possibly spend that much money?"

"Gambling."

Saoirse stopped crying. "How could he do this and just leave?"

"Are you really surprised?"

Saoirse shook her head. "No." She put her hair in her mouth and chewed on the end, a habit that Donnchadh had broken her of when she was 5. She only did it now when she was really stressed out.

"I'm trying to fix it," Donnchadh said, hating the word "try". It implied that there was a chance that he might fail.

"What am I going to do about

healer's training?"

"You might have to defer."

"They don't allow it. You know how many people apply every year. There are 100 people who apply per slot; they'd never hold one for me next year."

"Saoirse...we don't have a choice here."

"I'm going to murder Gairbith," Saoirse said.

"You'd never murder your brother, but Mr. Cross might murder you. I want you to stay in well-lit areas with a lot of people. It's probably best if you stay with Rhonwyn for the next few days."

"But her cat hates me! You know that his tail always goes up when he sees me. He might be pretty, but he's mean."

"Too bad." If Donnchadh was ready to dishonor himself to keep her safe, she could deal with a hostile cat.

"But he hates me!"

"Saoirse, do you want to die?"

"No."

"Then you'll do as I ask. Don't go anywhere alone right now. I'm trying to pay off the debt. I negotiated for 30% interest per month."

Saoirse choked. "No."

"I did. It was the only way for both of us to stay alive."

"Have they tried to kill you?"

"Define 'kill'."

"Donn! Stop playing around. Have they tried to hurt you?"

"Yes." Donnchadh looked at the new furniture. "They have. They got my roommate."

Saoirse gasped. "You're not safe even inside of the KSM base on Dalat? How could they reach you there?"

"My contact information is readily available to anybody who is offering a contract to KSM. You know that. I'm not going to be able to hide, and we no longer have the money to figure out a way for you to hide. You've just got to stay with Rhonwyn."

"I'll do it," Saoirse promised. "Maybe I'll bake cat treats or something."

"That sounds good," Donnchadh told her. "I'll figure out a way to get you some credits."

Right then, Giang's alarm went off. Saoirse covered her ears, so Donnchadh ended the call. They wouldn't be able to hear each other anymore. He went to shake Giang awake and dodged Giang's fist.

Spaceship Simulation

Donnchadh

"Get up. We have to be ready for simulations in 20."

Giang's speech was garbled since he was a half-dead zombie when he was first awoken, but he shambled towards his uniform and shoes. Donnchadh stifled a laugh when he saw that Giang's shoes were on the wrong feet. He'd catch a little grief during inspection, but he wouldn't be seriously hurt.

Donnchadh brought Giang to the commissary to grab a little bit of bánh bao before they went into training. They each took as many buns as they could carry and ate them while walking quickly to the training center.

They got there one minute before they needed to be there. Giang's eyes were finally starting to open, so Donnchadh hoped that he'd be able to function. There was a 50% chance that Giang would just keel over.

Today, they were playing with mock spaceships. They couldn't waste the fuel and maintenance of actual ships, but they would use them via 3D computers, not in physical space. They all strapped on their virtual reality helmets and began to shoot and dodge. The last one standing would be the one with under 50 hits. They were in a starscape that was littered with space debris. They could hide behind it, but their spacecraft could also be damaged by it if they came too close.

Donnchadh's flight skills always served him well in these simulations. He hid behind the planet in the starscape, waiting for everyone else to kill each other so that he'd be able to come in, finish off the last person, and be the last man standing. He couldn't see beyond the planet, but he kept his lasers ready to hit anybody who got the same bright idea as him.

Unfortunately, the person who came around the dark side of the planet was Horus. Horus wasn't expecting Donnchadh at all, so Donnchadh's lasers fired on him too quickly for him to properly shield. He scrambled for his shields and lasers at the same time and couldn't initiate either. Donnchadh quickly sent out 50 pulses, killing Horus and sending him out of the sim. He dodged Horus' dead spacecraft as it came hurtling towards him.

Finally, enough time had passed for Donnchadh to look beyond the planet, which he rose above. He could see that there were only two opponents left.

He wove his way over to their battleground as they dodged and shot each other. He was at their side and hitting them on their flanks, but he ducked right after every shot. They just thought that their visible opponent's lasers were hitting their sides; they didn't realize that Donnchadh was contributing to both of their hit counts.

Finally, both of their spaceships froze. They'd reached the 50 hit limit.

Donnchadh was the only one left.

He could feel someone pulling off his helmet. It was Giang, who grinned.

"Good job."

"Thank you."

"You're the worst winner ever," Horus sneered. "You just cheated and waited for everyone else to shoot at each other so you could win."

"I met you on the dark side of the planet, too, Horus, or have you forgotten?" Donnchadh replied. There was silence in the regiment. With a scowl, Horus let the matter drop.

Donnchadh didn't have time for

petty rivalries. He had much bigger fish to fry. If he wasn't careful, though, Horus would try to find ways to sabotage him on the base. He wouldn't have to worry about Mr. Cross's thugs gaining access if Horus tried anything. He was glad that Giang had insisted on getting a retina lock.

Giang's words had haunted him throughout the simulation. He could definitely use a friend. If he were back on Releon, he'd love to have someone to lean on. He'd been his family's bedrock for so long that he didn't know what it was like to have support. His father, now dead, had never been demonstrative or affectionate. He had vague memories of a loving mother, but she'd been gone so long now that he mostly remembered what she looked like from pictures. Saoirse had been a child — and was a child still — and Gairbith was the opposite of Donnchadh in many ways.

But dragging Giang into something that would have

repercussions on his family on Dalat would be unconscionable.

Donnchadh was already down in the mud, and he had no desire for any of his trouble to land in Giang's lap. He'd soldier on alone, because that's what he always did.

Advance

Donnchadh

Late at night, Donnchadh snuck
into the comptroller's office. He'd be
due a substantial amount of pay once
the contract for Ngo Xuong Xi was
fulfilled, but that didn't help him now
with the thugs at his door or
Saoirse's training.

Was it really so bad to provide for
his little sister? The comptroller
didn't advance pay for anybody, but

Donnchadh opened up his computer. The comptroller's password was his middle name — one of the least secure ideas ever — and Donnchadh quickly rearranged things so that he'd be paid some of his fee in advance. It was enough to pay for a year of training for Saoirse and maybe enough to pay a month's worth of interest on Gairbith's debt.

He was sweating. Was he really willing to commit financial fraud just for his little sister's dreams?

But he found himself clicking the

"Save" button, finalizing the payroll. He knew that it was sent to the bank exactly at midnight, which was why he hacked in at 23:58. There was no time to undo what he'd done. They'd just chalk it up to a computer error; the money would be paid to him anyway, on a different time schedule.

He cleaned up every trace that he'd been there, both in the physical world and the cyber world. The comptroller would never know what he'd done; there'd be no evidence to court-martial him for committing fraud.

Careful not to be seen, he went into the hallway and walked back to his own room. But the hallways were totally empty at this hour, and he made it back to his room without meeting a soul.

* * *

The next morning, Sergeant Park came to Donnchadh's room. Donnchadh's eyelids felt heavy from the lack of sleep, but he got up nonetheless when his CO came in. Giang was still snoring.

"Good morning, sir," he said slowly.

"The day after tomorrow is the big day, your first real assignment," the sergeant said in a loud voice that seemed louder than Giang's horrible alarm; Giang turned over and groaned. "Are you ready to transport Princess Celeste to her chosen mate?"

The sergeant was talking about it as if Princess Celeste had chosen to marry a pirate-dictator, not the other way around.

"Yes, sir."

"We've gotten more information than the initial dossier that we sent to you. It's on this card. Read it and follow it religiously. Believe me, you won't be disappointed by the size of the payment involved. Dismissed."

Sergeant Park walked out of the room. Donnchadh went to his tablet and swiped the card. He read through the information. Ngo Xuong Xi had given very specific instructions: the transporter needed to be a reliable cadet with battle experience, including experience through simulations, stellar pilot scores, and a solid command of intricate mapping, because the space system that he would be traveling through had a number of splintered off routes that must be traveled carefully if he was to deliver his charge according to the contract.

Donnchadh jumped a foot as Giang's alarm went off. They needed to get to the training center soon. He got dressed in his uniform and waited for Giang to stumble out of bed.

"Let's go."

Giang, instead of replying, just slowly walked toward the door. Donnchadh accompanied him to the commissary before their day began.

Party

Donnchadh

When the cadets finished their training for the day, they headed for the space bar. He ordered a shot of ruou, then he ordered another.

"What's up with you, Donnchadh? You normally don't drink that much."

"I got my first real assignment."

Giang slapped him on the back. "That's great news. Hey, everybody!"

he said, his voice cutting through the conversation and music in the space bar, "Donnchadh got his first assignment!"

All of the cadets in the bar cheered. There weren't that many — only the ones from Donnchadh's regiment — but they were all green. None of them had been sent on a real mission.

"This calls for a celebration. Let's open up the bubbly!"

All of the alcohol in the space bar was included, except for the

incredibly expensive Oxitan white
wine that was only used for
celebrations.

Donnchadh leaned in close before
Giang got carried away. "I can't afford
to buy enough bubbly for everyone."

Giang shook his head. "It's on
me."

Donnchadh was startled, his eyes
widening. Was Giang rich? He looked
him over, but all he saw was the
regulation uniform that everyone else
wore.

He shrugged. He'd accept Giang's

gift. He had already decided that he wouldn't drag Giang into his mess, but he did hope that he could one day enjoy Giang's closer friendship...if he returned from this first mission. He'd tell Giang the truth once it was over, once he had fixed up the tangled mess that Gairbith had created for his family.

One bottle of bubbly was followed by two bottles of bubbly. For some reason, the rest of the cadets took special pleasure in keeping Donnchadh's glass full, probably because he normally drank very little. It felt like a repeat of his 21st birthday again. He let them refill his glass again and again, hoping to find the solution for the unease in his stomach at the bottom of his glass, unease which stemmed from not really wanting to drop a helpless girl off for Ngo Xuong Xi to marry. No matter how many times he drained it, the solution never came. He was stuck.

He drank until Donnchadh felt the burn of vomit in the back of his throat. He got to his feet and noticed that the room was moving around him. He put his hand on his chair to stay upright.

"Whoa, there," Giang said, putting a steadying hand on his back. "Okay, marines, let's pack it up and call it a night. Donnchadh can't stand anymore." The rest of them drained their glasses and walked back to their quarters, some more steadily than others.

Giang put Donnchadh's arm around his shoulders before he

pulled and half-carried Donnchadh back to their room. Giang was much stronger than he looked. He was compact with the muscles of a fighter, which meant that he weighed about 50 more librae than a normal Releon male of his size.

He finally wrestled Donnchadh into bed. Donnchadh's eyes were closed, and he began to hiccup as Giang brought their waste receptacle next to Donnchadh's bunk.

"Throw up in here if you need it."

Donnchadh was too far gone to

even reply. His eyelids felt like they

weighed 500 librae, and he quickly

fell asleep.

Painkillers

Donnchadh

Donnchadh woke up to feel vomit burning his throat. He barely turned over in time to deposit it right into the waste receptacle that Giang had strategically placed last night. His roommate was still sleeping off the alcohol, peacefully snoring away. Giang had probably had about half of what Donnchadh had drunk last night.

Donnchadh got out of bed, even though his head felt as if it were stuffed with cotton and his mouth was dry. He opened up his med-kit, which came standard for every space marine. He found the bottle of simple painkillers; on the back, the pills contained a list of instructions. Someone his weight should take two every twelve hours. He popped 6 to get rid of the pounding in his head, swallowing them dry.

Too soon, he'd be on a spaceship to transport the princess and bring her to a husband whom she had never met.

Somehow, without drinking himself to death, he was going to have to get over it and do the mission without feeling the guilt. He could worry about Princess Celeste, but his little sister was more important. Princess Celeste was going to marry a wealthy and powerful man; surely that wasn't the worst fate in the universe. His sister's life was at stake. Donnchadh cared much less about his own life than Saoirse's.

He'd stay in KSM forever if it meant that she'd be safe, but it was obvious that she wouldn't be until he could pay off Mr. Cross.

He hopped into the sonic shower and quickly cleaned up before putting on his uniform. He still felt horrible, but he thought that the vomiting was done, at least.

After he'd done his routine of pulling Giang out of bed, the two of them swiped breakfast from the commissary and went to the day's training exercise. Today, they needed to find a black box that contained secrets that KSM needed to retrieve. Donnchadh hadn't had the chance to touch it, so he needed to find it the old-fashioned way, through diligent searching. He partnered with Giang, and the two of them scoured the set of buildings where it was hidden. The first ones to find the box would be let off early from training that day. The rest of them would have to do PT for the rest of the day. It was enough of an incentive to make the marines force others to stay away from their newly declared "territory."

Donnchadh closed his eyes. He tried to think like one of their instructors. If he wanted to make it difficult but not impossible to find the black box, where would he hide it?

Of course. It would be in a nearly inaccessible place. He knew where the least inaccessible place was in this set of buildings, because they often trained here.

"Come on," he told Giang.

"Where are we going?"

"To get the box."

"But everyone's searching over here."

"It's not here."

"I thought that you could only find things that you'd touched?"

"True."

"So why are you pulling me away from where everyone else is looking?"

"Because they're approaching this in the wrong way. It's not about finding the black box. It's about thinking like the instructors."

Giang nodded. "Got you." He followed Donnchadh then as

Donnchadh crept around a building out of sight. The two of them quietly slipped towards the power generators that powered the buildings.

During their second month, they'd been trained in the art of working with electronics. Donnchadh had learned very little about computers, since he knew quite a bit already, but he'd been fascinated by the idea of electricity and what exactly could be done with it. One wire going haywire just once could bring an entire spaceship to a standstill; in deep space, an unfixable engine problem was certain death unless they could call for help or launch their emergency life ship to a nearby planet. There were emergency call systems, but the only one that wasn't electronic was something that the ancients had called a "signal flare". It consisted of throwing a sparkling fire into space and hoping that someone saw it before it burned out. Donnchadh knew that if he sent a signal flare, the odds would be grim. Space was a very large place.

So he'd paid attention, learning about the mechanics of the spaceships that he would steer during his time working for KSM. They had a standard set of spaceships so that every marine could handle every spaceship that KSM had in its fleet. They hired other people to fly if they ever had specialized needs, but their spaceships were appropriate in 99% of situations, especially since KSM focused on extractions and delivery. Their needs were nearly always the same, which meant that the spaceships they had were the best for what they did.

Donnchadh ignored the warning signs on the power generator room's doors and walked right in.

"What are you doing?" Giang said, standing in the doorway and looking over his shoulder. "We aren't allowed to be in here."

"Do you want to win? Then just follow my lead."

With another glance over his shoulder, Giang stepped into the room.

Black Box

Donnchadh

Donnchadh moved forward to look at the generators. He opened one of the panels. Inside, they had a medley of wires, wires it had taken him nearly a month to master. And just as he had suspected, there was a small black box behind the wires.

It was a tricky puzzle. If he simply reached in and got out the black box, he'd be electrocuted and dead before the KSM healers even got a chance to see him. But if he cut the power to the wires, then electricity would go out for this training area and possibly in part of the base.

"How are we going to get the box?" Giang whispered. "Do you have rubber gloves or something?"

"No gloves," Donnchadh said. The instructors would never give them an impossible task, so there had to be something here that would be safe for him to use.

When he turned around, he saw

what the instructors had left. He smiled.

"Why are you smiling?" Giang looked over his shoulder. "Oh!"

"They thought of everything." Donnchadh moved to take the small battery pack and rubber bag. He spliced together the line as he'd been taught by his instructors, which was tricky business. In ideal circumstances, he wouldn't be doing this so close to a live wire, but these weren't ideal circumstances. He finally succeeded in putting the battery's power supply next to the generators. It wouldn't have that much juice, but it would probably have enough to keep the lights on until Donnchadh could power up the generator again.

He flicked the switch to bring the generator to a halt. The glowing blue light, the one that meant that the power was on, turned off. The portable battery was already down to 40%. It wasn't made to withstand the power needs of a training center.

"Right," Donnchadh said. "Let's

get this puppy out." Without cutting any wires, he put on the rubber bag as if it were a mitten and reached inside of the generator. He could feel warmth, but he wasn't going to die of electrocution — not today, anyway.

He got the small black box out, dropping it only once before he could get it out from behind the wires.

"The battery's down to 5%." Donnchadh looked over at the battery; the display was red and flashing a warning message.

"Time to get this generator back

up." Donnchadh flipped the switch and watched as the generator initiated again. He went to unplug the battery from the power supply and threw the small black box at Giang.

"Crazy to go through all this just for the black box, marine."

"Sometimes you've got to take a little risk to get a reward, Giang."

Giang held onto the box as he and Donnchadh walked back to their starting point. Their sergeant was there, eating an apple. He choked when he saw the black box in Giang's hand.

"You found it already? Stars above, nobody's ever found it in less than 2 hours. Did you ask somebody where it would be?"

"No, sir."

Sergeant Park's face showed that he didn't believe it, but he held out his hand for the small black box in any case. Giang gave it to him.

He inspected it.

"Seems to be the right one." He put the black box onto a small white rectangle. The black box began to play a hologram.

"Is that Cloaked, sir?"

"Yes, it is. One of my favorite shows, you know. I thought about becoming an agent myself, but KSM suited me better." He winked at Giang and Donnchadh. "Go on, now. I'm going to punish the rest of your brothers for the rest of the afternoon. Better escape while you can."

Giang and Donnchadh nearly sprinted away from the training area. Sergeant Park's threats weren't idle. He'd put them into PT despite their recovery and delivery of the black box.

"What do you want to do this afternoon?"

"I don't know...spar I guess. There's not much else to do besides get drunk, and after last night, I don't think that's a good idea. You're a lightweight."

Donnchadh outweighed Giang by probably 100 librae, so he elbowed him so hard that Giang was forced to take a side-step.

"Lightweight?"

"When it comes to alcohol," Giang amended.

"Let's spar," Donnchadh sighed. Maybe fighting would take his mind off of what he was about to do.

While they walked to the sparring room, Donnchadh thought about the simulation. He wished that KSM's normal work involved recovery and destruction or delivery of secrets without seeing what information was contained inside. He felt better about that kind of work than probing, kidnapping, and delivering helpless females. It was the sort of work that would actually have meaning for him, but he was stuck on his course. And it wouldn't be all bad. He'd ensure Saoirse's safety with just one mission, and his conscience would just have to be satisfied with that level of heroism.

Fight

Donnchadh

Giang and Donnchadh were covered in sweat by the time that the other cadets left their training and came to the sparring room. Donnchadh was very glad that he'd been able to dodge it this time around. It was uncomfortable to stagger around the base like a sheep with the staggers when his legs were as sore as they got after training. He could see the other cadets moving gingerly, knowing that the worst would come tomorrow and the day after.

Horus was with them, apparently not sore at all. He really did have to be using performance-enhancing drugs, but how could he? KSM did regular drug tests on all of their employees; the nano-bots could report on the health of their normal hosts. Donnchadh understood now that KSM's nano-bots were about more than probing; they were a way to keep tabs on their marines. There were no deserters when it came to KSM.

"Star child," Horus sneered. "Always got to be the best, don't you?"

Donnchadh didn't say anything. It wasn't his fault that his comrades had focused on the wrong spot and looked at the challenge in the wrong way.

Donnchadh's silence ticked Horus off even more. He came over and pushed Donnchadh's chest, making him step backward one step.

"Do you think that you're so special because you're the first one in your regiment to transport some bimbo to her husband-to-be?"

Right as he said the last word, Donnchadh felt something snap inside of his chest. All the fear and worry came bubbling to the surface, and he found his right fist crashing into Horus' jaw. Horus fell to the floor, and Donnchadh sat on top of him, pinning Horus' arms with his knees and using Horus' face as a punching bag, alternating strikes between fists. It was much more satisfying to use his face than any speed bag.

Too soon, he could feel Giang and the other cadets pulling him off of Horus. Donnchadh noticed with satisfaction that Horus' nose was just a little crooked now. A small trickle of blood was coming out of it.

"Stop it, marine. We can't let the commander see you beat one of us."

Donnchadh shook his fist, feeling the pain from his raw knuckles now.

He looked and saw just a small smidgen of blood on his middle knuckle with a few drops on his other knuckles. He didn't know if it was from him or Horus, nor did he care.

He looked at Horus, who was staring at him from the floor. An instant of silent communication passed between them, and Donnchadh understood that Horus wouldn't be reporting the incident. It would offend his prideful nature and get both of them in trouble. In some strange way, finally getting to beat the smug bastard had released some of his tension and earned him Horus' respect at the same time, even though he'd behaved unprofessionally.

"Let's go back to our room, Donnchadh. You need to wrap your hand."

He looked back down. The blood on his knuckles had increased; the blood was definitely coming from him.

Waving goodbye to the other cadets, Donnchadh walked with Giang back to their room. Giang swiped antibacterial cleanser on Donnchadh's hand before wrapping it.

"I can do it myself," Donnchadh protested.

"Not as well as I can do it. You know that I'm here for you? Just take the two seconds of help from someone else, brother."

Donnchadh didn't know what to say to that. He'd relied on himself for so long that it felt weird to have someone else bandage him up. The last person he could remember caring for him was his mother. He smiled at what Giang would think of the comparison.

"What are you smiling about?"

"Nothing," he said, his grin broadening. "Thank you for fixing me up."

"Anytime, soldier. I'm going to take a sonic shower now."

"Sounds good."

Giang opened his trunk to bring out his nightwear and disappeared into their bathroom. Donnchadh leaned back in his bunk, opening his tablet so that he could access the file that he had on Princess Celeste and his mission.

Nav Cards

Donnchadh

The next morning, he left his
room before Giang's alarm went off.
He was scheduled to be on his ship
before breakfast. He knew that a crew
would have already provisioned his
ship, so he didn't need to worry about
breakfast. He had a travel bag that
held his most prized possessions. He
still had the stuffed animal that
Saoirse had made for him when she

was three in preschool. It was a small lopsided frog with his name "embroidered" on it in her child's handwriting, but it always made him smile. Along with the frog, he had a ring from his father that he kept in a jewelry box. His father might be dead, but Donnchadh knew that his father always meant for his mother's ring to end up on Donnchadh's bride's hand. He also knew that his marriage wouldn't be anytime soon. His life was a mess, and there were almost no females on Dalat, let alone single ones.

If he didn't come back, he wouldn't care about the rest of his stuff in his room. Eventually, it might go to Saoirse, but he didn't know if he minded the officers just throwing it away or giving it to the janitorial staff to clean up.

He finally got to the docks about ten minutes before his flight slot. The dock was empty at this hour. Everything was handled by robots when the base was asleep.

He held his eye open as the

retina lock identified him and opened the door to his spacecraft.

When he walked inside, he let out a low whistle. They'd given him a spacecraft that was top of the line. Not a single one of KSM's spacecraft was shabby, but this one was so far in the opposite direction that he felt like a prince. They'd spared no expense when it came to this spaceship, and he realized now how much support and pull Ngo Xuong Xi had. They wanted him to succeed with this mission as it would help their long-term objectives on Dalat.

He went to the control panel, which lit as he came near it. It must've had motion detectors instead of the standard ignition. There were navigation cards on his chair, just waiting to be swiped through the computer when his journey began. He swiped them quickly and sat in his seat. The metal straps twisted around him again as the ship took off. This spaceship was much nicer than the one that he'd handled for his test run and the ones that he saw in his simulations. It must be a newer make, because there were a few buttons that he didn't recognize, even though KSM made a point to train every cadet on every ship's controls during simulations.

When the pressure eased, he got out of his seat and looked around the ship. He couldn't stop his jaw from dropping as he saw the small water shower in the corner of the bathroom. He had the standard sonic shower, of course, but water showers were only for the wasteful and ludicrously rich.

He'd rather drink water than bathe in it. In fact, he'd never had the money for a water shower. His father probably hadn't ever had one, either. Water was money, and though they'd been provided for during their childhood, a frivolous waste of money was never going to be condoned in his father's household.

Instead of the capsules that had served as bedrooms on the other ship, he had two true bedrooms, one slightly larger than the other. They had small bunks in them with the same metal straps that the chairs next to the control panel had. He guessed that those would be used if someone were sleeping while the ship landed.

Going into the main area again, he saw that he had a small kitchen. He opened the drawers to see enough meals to last him a month and a food replicator that said that it could produce 1,000 meals before needing to be refilled. How long was this trip supposed to last, again? Maybe he'd try to make it last forever.

The nagging feeling in his gut hadn't gone away, but he tried to assuage it by justifying what he was doing. For all he knew, the bride could desperately want to marry Ngo Xuong Xi and was madly in love with him. Maybe there were hard conditions on her planet and her marriage could save her people, the Elysians. He hadn't spent much time with Ngo Xuong Xi, so maybe there was a good man beneath the fierce and game-playing exterior.

Donnchadh knew that he was

lying to himself, but he made sure that the ship was on course before going into the smaller bedroom and closing his eyes. Soon, he'd be near Oxitan and ready to complete the first phase of his mission.

Makeover

Celeste

"Ouch! You're poking me in the eye."

The makeup artist was absolutely unrepentant. "Don't move when I'm doing your waterline. Look up."

Celeste suppressed a sigh and looked up. She had no idea why she was suddenly surrounded by a hairdresser, a makeup artist, and a personal stylist. Her stepfather didn't believe in frivolous waste, unless it was for his own daughters, and Celeste had gone without cosmetics for so long that she barely knew how to apply them herself. It always irritated her stepsisters that Celeste's skin glowed more than theirs did and was softer, despite the fact that she couldn't buy the same creams and potions that they used for their skin.

"What is all of this for?"

Nobody would answer her, instead they chattered among themselves about the best way to coordinate everything for the best possible effect.

Finally, after what felt like an eternity, they were done poking her. The stylist untied Celeste's robe and invaded her personal space by slipping it off of her shoulders. She was wearing a deep red dress, one that was the color of aged wine. Her dark hair was up in an elegant twist while a small circlet of rubies was set in her hair, nearly cemented in with hairspray.

"Good enough," the makeup

artist said. "Don't smudge anything."

The three of them left Celeste alone in

her room. She went to her dresser,

which had a mirror attached to it.

Celeste had to admit that the

woman in the mirror looked both

older and sexier than Celeste actually

was. She had been kept away from

her people ever since her mother,

Queen Ariane, had married her

stepfather, Oxarex. In a matriarchal

society, women were supposed to

rule, but Oxarex had somehow

convinced her mother to put most of

the power into her hands, which was unusual for a consort. Celeste didn't know what would happen when her mother died, but she was next in line for the throne as the crown princess. Somehow, she doubted that her stepfather would readily give up all the power that he'd taken from her mother.

She stopped looking at herself with her fancy hair, makeup, and clothing, and turned so that she could stare through her windows at her kingdom below. The Elysians had barely seen their crown princess for years, locked up as she was. Oxarex had told her mother and Celeste that they needed to stay inside for their own safety, but he left the castle every day. Celeste had to admit that her enforced homestay had placed a toll on her.

But Celeste hadn't changed as much as her mother. Celeste could still remember her childhood. Her parents had been deeply in love before Celeste's father, Queen Ariane's consort, Thibault, had died in a sudden summer illness. Oxarex was a healer who had visited her father every day during his convalescence, and every day Thibault had grown worse. Oxarex was Ariane's shoulder to cry on during that difficult time, and before Celeste's father was barely cold in his grave, Oxarex had convinced Queen Ariane to marry him. Celeste had thrown a tantrum when her mother broke the news, but nothing she'd said, the spoiled 12-year-old brat that she'd been, had swayed her mother's decision.

And so Celeste had grown into a young woman under Oxarex's thumb. His daughters were given every comfort and open purses; they could move around Elysia as much as they liked. In contrast, Celeste had stayed inside to learn about anything that she could possibly be taught. She learned music, languages, history, science, and any other thing for which her mother could find a teacher. Queen Ariane emphasized that Celeste needed to know all that she could to become the best ruler that she could be once Celeste ascended to the throne, so Celeste had learned every day until she felt like her brain was overstuffed.

When someone knocked on the door, Celeste turned away from the window.

"Yes?"

"Your presence is required for dinner."

Why was her steward sweating?

"Did you run here?"

"No, Your Highness."

Celeste frowned. Something was wrong. She could just feel it.

Feast

Celeste

The steward brought Celeste into the formal dining hall, the one that they only used for formal occasions. When they were dining en famille, they used their smaller breakfast chamber. Celeste rubbed the back of her neck. Something was going on, and she didn't like it.

The feeling grew stronger as she entered the room. The table was practically groaning with the quantity of food on it; it was filled edge to edge in covered platters. The smell was incredible and made Celeste's stomach grumble. It was enough food to feed thirty people or more, and her family only had five people: her mother, herself, her stepfather, and his idiotic daughters. They were already there. Her mother seemed a little surprised to see how dressed up Celeste was, but she said nothing. Oxarex had a way of shutting her mother down any time that she spoke, and Celeste had to admit that Oxarex's cutting comments made her blood boil. Celeste could take the emotional abuse, but hurting her mother was like kicking a newborn kitten, since her mother was a gentle soul who would never defend herself.

Oxarex obviously had planned something, but what? He'd never answer her directly if she asked him straight out. She'd have to irritate him into telling her what was going on.

For several weeks, Oxarex had

been behaving strangely. Celeste had entered the throne room once to catch him whispering to a man over his Holo Comm, a newfangled glow pad. Celeste had never liked or trusted Oxarex, including when her father was alive, and her instincts were tingling.

The steward pulled out Celeste's chair. She seated herself carefully, sweeping her skirts so that they wouldn't wrinkle. As soon as her chair was pushed in, their bots began to open the covered plates.

Everything was the finest and most expensive food that they could get. Nearly everything on the table was imported, and every dish was exactly what Oxarex liked. What was going on? It was as if tonight's dinner were a celebration, but there wasn't anything to celebrate.

Celeste indicated to one of the bots that she wanted to eat the écrevisse, which was her favorite food. She nearly moaned as the salty flavor burst upon her tongue. It was covered in a rich butter sauce with plenty of herbs in it, and Celeste considered herself lucky that Oxarex enjoyed something that Celeste adored.

Oxarex was pontificating at the head of the table on the export of their violettes double — he had talked to the producers about growing more flowers, and they were deliberately disobeying — when Celeste cut him off. His eyes flashed as she talked over him.

"So, Oxarex, what are you celebrating?"

He only smiled. "Can't I just enjoy a wonderful night with my lovely family? Is that too hard to believe?"

"Only if I were as stupid as your daughters."

Oxarex and his daughters gasped. Hortense and Manon chimed together, "How rude!"

Oxarex, however, refused to be provoked into saying anything about what was going on. He only smiled at her, aggravating her even further.

Celeste looked down at her plate,

her appetite lost, even though she very rarely had the opportunity to eat écrevisse. She hated to waste food, especially astronomically expensive food bought by the royal treasury, but she couldn't eat another bite. She looked at her mother.

Queen Ariane looked troubled. In her younger days, she would have scolded Princess Celeste for conduct unbecoming a future monarch. Now, though, she didn't say a word.

It hurt Princess Celeste's heart to see how silent her mother was. She'd lost her spirit to Oxarex's machinations, slowly at first, but quickly once he had gained the upper hand.

Celeste hated Oxarex with a passion for stealing the kingdom and her mother's spirit.

And he hated her back.

Opera Invitation

Celeste

At the end of the meal, the bots
closed the plates and moved all the
food away from the dinner table. They
served little demitasses of tea, which
they sipped quietly. In other
households, including her own when
her father Thibault was alive, the
after-dinner ritual of tea was bonding
time. In this household, it was just
an uncomfortable time of awkward

silence.

Oxarex broke it by asking Celeste, "Do you still like the opera?"

Celeste blinked at him. She hadn't been permitted to go to the opera for years; Oxarex had cited security concerns and the cost of keeping a royal box, which was funny, since Oxarex spent freely on himself and his daughters. Her father had loved to sing, and she'd had all kinds of music lessons as a child and as a young woman. The opera was something that brought together two things which she dearly loved: music and stories.

"Yes." Celeste tried not to hope that there was something good that would come out of this very strange night. Could he be trying to gain her trust for some reason? No. Considering his behavior at dinner, Celeste knew that he was not worried whether or not she trusted him. He was up to something. She could feel it in her bones.

"I reserved a box for you tonight." Celeste tried not to let her jaw touch the floor. Why would her stingy stepfather give her something that she loved beyond all measure? The opera transported her into a place beyond her cloistered life inside of the Elysian palace, and he was offering her a tiny escape, a gift.

"Can my mother come with me?" After all, their family used to sing Celeste's lullabies together when they tucked her into her bed, a little nightly ritual that brought the three of them closer together. Celeste couldn't remember the last time that she'd heard her mother sing.

"No." Oxarex's tone showed that Celeste couldn't try to negotiate for her mother to come too. A box certainly had room for more than one person, but Celeste didn't want to push her luck. She could barely believe that he'd let her go to the opera.

Was an outing to the opera part of his plan? If it was, then she doubted that she was actually at risk. He was a spineless man, and anything that he'd put together was sure to fall apart, anyway. He'd done a terrible job of running the kingdom, and only the near-monopoly that Oxitan had on flowers kept them afloat despite his financial mismanagement.

"Your levi-car will meet you outside, Celeste. Kiss your mother goodbye."

Celeste rose to her feet, her heart beating fast. She wished that she'd kept a knife concealed in her dress. She hadn't had the chance to grab one. Her father had believed in equality between the sexes, possibly because he existed in a matriarchal society, and Celeste had received early weapons training every week until Thibault had died. Then everything had stopped.

She went to her mother and kissed the top of her head, sniffing her mother's perfume, which smelled like roses with dew on them. She loved her mother with her whole heart, and she hugged her hard. Queen Ariane hugged her back with so much force that Celeste realized that her mother had been starved of affection for a long time. If nothing happened tonight at the opera, Celeste would make a point to be affectionate with her mother more often. A simple hug or kiss on the cheek could go a long way towards making her mother feel a little less lonely. Though she was the ruler in name, it was a hollow power. She had less say than Celeste did.

But Celeste could not solve that problem tonight, so she curtsied to her step-family before going to the front of the palace for her levi-car.

Budget Levi-Car

Celeste

When she got to the front, she was severely disappointed by the big levi-car that awaited her. It looked like it was older than she was, rust on some panels, paint peeling on others. Why was she so dressed up for a hideous levi-car like this? It didn't seem to fit.

Of course Oxarex would pay for the cheapest levi-car that he could.

Maybe her mother had finally spoken up for once and they'd had an argument, an argument which Oxarex was trying to solve by letting Celeste go to the opera. It would explain her mother's behavior at dinner.

Shaking her thoughts aside, Celeste entered the levi-car, glad that she'd opted for low heels.

She was taken aback when she saw that she had company. They drove themselves, so why was there a man in her car?

He was undeniably gorgeous with a shock of long flame-colored hair that was the exact shade that Celeste adored. It was the color of sunshine and fire at the same time, multiple colors and shades.

He didn't say a word, but she looked into his crystal blue eyes. They said that the eyes were the window to the soul, and Celeste saw his; she was the slightest bit telepathic, and she got the ability from her father. Her mother and Oxarex had no idea that some of the thoughts in their heads came from her, and she wanted to keep it that way. She knew that he was a warrior with a good heart, so she relaxed just a fraction. She leaned back in her seat and closed her eyes as she remembered the last time that she'd been to the opera. She'd been a young girl then, pre-pubescent, and her stomach was bubbling with excitement as she thought of sitting in a nice box and viewing the whole thing. She replayed each moment in her head.

* * *

She must have fallen asleep, because she woke up and had to wipe a bit of drool from the corner of her mouth. She looked outside of the window of the levi-car. Wherever they were, she couldn't recognize it.

"Where are we?"

"Don't worry about it."

Being told not to worry about it made her heart thump wildly in her chest.

"I want you to take me home immediately!" She glared at him. Her telepathic powers had let her down; she no longer thought that she was going to the opera.

"Relax."

Celeste was the furthest from being relaxed that she'd ever been. She tried to control the panic rising in her chest, but it was a fruitless fight.

"What's going on?"

"I'm just doing my job, Your Highness." He sighed. "It couldn't have been comfortable to sleep in your seat. Why don't you sleep on the bed in the back until we get to your destination?"

What a strange way to talk about her trip to the opera. It made her feel strange and a little confused. She couldn't imagine why they were taking the long route to the opera, and to be frank, she had no idea where she was. She didn't have the best sense of direction in normal situations, and she was even worse off when she'd slept through the journey. She hadn't been out in Elysia in a long time, so she had no idea what the roads were named. Even if she somehow jumped out of the levi-car — doubtful given the security measures in place even in the oldest levi-cars — she wouldn't be able to find her way. She might as well get some rest.

"Fine," she spat. "But I'm not happy."

The man said nothing in reply, but she saw a shadow cross his face. She hoped that he felt bad about whatever he was doing to her.

She went into the bedroom and

kicked off her shoes before she lay down in the bed. The man was at her doorway now.

"No peeking," she teased. She actually wouldn't mind a moment or two with him, gorgeous as he was; she hadn't had much of a chance to dally with anybody, virtually trapped in the palace as she'd been for so long.

He wasn't peeking, it turned out. Before Celeste could react, the door to the bedroom was shut and locked. Celeste heard a thud as the bolt slotted into place. She tried to turn it,

but she saw that there was a third

lock, a retina lock on the outside.

Damsel in Distress

Donnchadh

"Let me out!" the lovely princess on the other side of the door screamed. He heard a thud as if she'd kicked the door. It was made of metal, though, and the princess was not large. He doubted that she could even dent the door, let alone kick it down.

Donnchadh's heart was troubled. Even putting her extreme beauty aside, as he should do to stay professional, he still worried about what he was doing. He'd never treat Saoirse like this, not even for her own good. He wasn't so cold that he could ignore the fact that the princess was in distress. The lies that he'd tried to tell himself to comfort his conscience were quickly disproven. Princess Celeste didn't have the faintest idea of the future that awaited her.

There was nothing in the mission file that stated that Princess Celeste needed to be kept in the dark. The mission was simply to deliver the virgin princess to Ngo Xuong Xi. Surely he wouldn't be reprimanded for telling her what was going on.

"Stop kicking the door," he told her. "I'll tell you what's going on."

"You better!" she screeched.

"You've been sold to a warlord."

"What!" Celeste hit the door again. "What are you talking about?"

Her volume was almost loud enough to make Donnchadh cover his ears.

"I said that you've been sold to a

Yuenanren warlord."

"You mean the people of Dalat? Oxitan's former colony?"

"Yes."

The next sound that Donnchadh heard was the sound of the porcelain vase inside of the bedroom breaking against the door. He winced. He'd tried to go for some kind of feminine touch, so he had picked up some Oxitan blooms while he was on planet. Obviously, the effort was not appreciated.

"I'll make you pay for this,"

Princess Celeste swore.

Time for Plan B. If Princess Celeste had gone willingly with him, he wouldn't have to resort to these measures.

Donnchadh headed for his gear, putting on his breathing mask. He took out a grenade full of sleeping gas and detonated it right outside of the bedroom door. Celeste's thumps on the door got slower and slower until he knew that she was asleep.

"I'm sorry, princess. It's my job."

He unlocked the door, finally,

and picked up her lovely form. She
had curves in all the right places, and
he couldn't deny that she felt good in
his arms. The levi-car stopped
moving, and Donnchadh knew that
they'd arrived back at his spaceship,
the one that KSM had given him to
complete the mission of delivering the
princess. She'd be out for another
hour at least, possibly more. She was
much smaller than Donnchadh. He
knew that the gas, if inhaled, would
put him to sleep for an hour, so
perhaps it would work on her for two.

He carried her into the ship, laying her gently in the larger bedroom so that she could sleep. She was lovely when she was sleeping, her long lashes touching the tops of her cheeks, her chest moving steadily up and down as she breathed slowly.

Donnchadh had to stop watching her. She was destined for Ngo Xuong Xi, no matter how beautiful she seemed. He closed the door to the bedroom, not bothering to retina lock it since she was on the KSM ship now, set their course for Dalat using the nav cards, and went to his own

bedroom to get some rest, too.

Sabotage

Celeste

When Celeste woke up, she was on a soft bed, but she was in a different room. She got to her feet. Her makeup had smudged onto the pillowcase. She didn't envy whoever had to clean it. She wandered around until she found the bathroom. After taking off her dress, she let the sonic shower take care of everything. She wasn't used to wearing a lot of makeup, and it felt weird to wake up with it on her face.

When she was clean, she put back on her dress, since she had no other clothes; when she left for the opera, she didn't know that she'd be going off-planet. She walked around the central area, seeing the control area, the other doors, the small kitchen, and the doorway which would lead her straight into space.

She sighed. Despite being angry, she wasn't completely suicidal. She wasn't about to spacewalk to get out of this mess. It seemed like the coward's way out.

She opened one door to find the warrior asleep inside. If he wasn't up, then she had a few more precious minutes of freedom.

Time to do some damage.

She walked to the back end of the spaceship, where the engines and power came from. She easily opened a panel on the power core. Yes, that's what she wanted. The wires were confusing, but she was pretty sure that she could stop this ship mid-space if she wanted to.

And she did.

So she pulled all of them, then Celeste started kicking the generator as it went off, hoping that she'd caused some damage inside of the generator itself. She knew that the pod needed to have some kind of emergency escape mechanism to meet intergalactic standards, so they wouldn't die. They'd still be able to figure something out.

Soon, the engines ground to a halt. The lights went off. Celeste grinned.

Perfect.

She went back into her room and slept again, this time a natural sleep instead of a gas-induced one.

Fury

Donnchadh

Donnchadh opened his eyes to near-complete darkness. There were emergency strips glowing just enough for Donnchadh to be able to see the way to the door.

He opened his door and went into the common area. It was dark too, the emergency strips a little bit darker there.

The power was out. Totally out.

He grabbed a portable light from his room, then he made his way to the back of the ship.

What greeted him was an open panel with a bunch of crossed wires. His mouth went dry as he thought about putting all of it back together. He could rewire things, true, but it would take time. With the engines off, they were free-floating in space, which was never a good thing.

He held the portable light in his teeth nonetheless. The faster he could put everything together, the better this mission would go. He didn't want to free-float for so long that KSM had to send someone to find him. It would be too embarrassing.

But even when all the wires were appropriately attached, nothing happened when he pressed the power button. Princess Celeste had done something.

Princess Celeste was turning out to be just as annoying as Saoirse when she put her mind to it...possibly worse. He headed towards her bedroom, where she was sleeping the deep sleep of the innocent. He shook her awake. Unlike Giang, she came awake instantly. Seeing a man in her room made her scream.

Donnchadh covered his ears.

"Stars above, princess! If I wanted to hurt you, I would've done it by now."

"That's true."

"What did you do?"

The portable light showed the gleam of her white teeth when she said, "Fixed things."

"I'm pretty sure you broke the ship."

"Good."

"Good?" Donnchadh yelped. "How is this good? We're going to die in this ship." Saoirse would die, too, and Gairbith whenever he surfaced.

"Don't be so dramatic," Princess Celeste said. "We have an emergency pod, don't we, to comply with intergalactic standards?"

"No."

"What?"

"This ship is built to be

lightweight and nimble. It isn't

equipped with an emergency pod. It's

built for stealth and speed, not safety.

KSM has a special permit from the

Intergalactic Federation to go without

emergency pods."

"Stars above," Princess Celeste

said. Her face was stricken, and

Donnchadh was glad that she

realized that she'd killed them both.

"Is there anything that we can do?"

"We have no juice left, thanks to

you. We can try to guide the

spaceship using its current

momentum, but there are no guarantees."

Princess Celeste's face had turned green.

"Where can we guide the spaceship to?"

Donnchadh thought about it. He'd normally use the ship's navigation systems, but without power, the high-tech map would be utterly useless. He'd have to do it by hand while steering. KSM's simulations had not prepared him for a feisty suicidal and homicidal princess.

"We might be able to find a place to dock if it's very close."

"How?"

"KSM keeps paper star charts in every ship under the console. It's an anachronism from a long time ago, but it's going to save our lives today. No thanks to you." He bent to get the paper maps out and spread them out on the seat beside him, looking for their quadrant.

"I'm sorry, okay? No need to keep making me feel bad."

"You've decreased our chances of living another day," Donnchadh exploded. "You're the most spoiled brat I've ever met."

"I'm not spoiled," Princess Celeste shouted back at him, stomping her foot. "I don't want to be forced to marry some gross, crusty warlord."

"One, he's not gross and crusty. He's the most powerful man on Dalat. Two, KSM issues refunds if the Bride delivered doesn't do the trick. In a year, you could be sent home."

"Oh. But I still don't want to live

for a year with a stranger."

"Tell me that your life on Oxitan was better."

Princess Celeste was quiet.

"That's what I thought. We do our research before we extract people."

"Extract? More like abduct."

"You cannot honestly tell me you had better prospects on your home planet. I read your file. Your mother is Queen Ariane, but the kingdom of Elysia is truly run by her consort, Oxarex. You've been living the life of a virtual hermit ever since your mother remarried; why would you throw away a chance to break free?"

"Because I love my mother," she said quietly.

Donnchadh felt his heart twist at her words. His own mother was gone, and he'd pay everything he had — which was not that much at this point — just to spend another day with her. He'd stolen this princess away from her family.

To distract himself from that disturbing thought, he checked the star charts to see their position. They were in luck. They were only about a mile away from a space station where they could dock and repair the ship.

Donnchadh forced the ship to turn a few degrees so that they'd land at the nearby space station. Their spaceship was going to take its sweet time, however, with no power.

"There's no point in waiting out here," Donnchadh told Princess Celeste. "Go and get some sleep. That way you won't think about how we might die."

Princess Celeste's lower lip

trembled, making Donnchadh feel like a total heel. She spun around and walked away from him without a word, slamming the door to her room.

Women. Donnchadh was glad that he wasn't involved with Princess Celeste, absolutely beautiful as she was. He'd seen her now with expertly applied makeup and totally fresh-faced, and he had to say that he preferred the latter. He had no idea why someone as pretty as Princess Celeste would even need the enhancement of makeup.

But despite her innate beauty, he wasn't ready for so much pepper in his bed. His entanglements, when he had them, were brief affairs to scratch an itch for both of them and nothing more. KSM's training had made him into a better lover, he knew, but he hadn't had a chance to test them on a living, breathing female.

The thought of probing Princess Celeste made his temperature spike. He knew that Ngo Xuong Xi had requested a virgin, so there wouldn't be any probing at all. He had to admit

that he wondered what Princess

Celeste looked like under her clothes,

but it would remain a mystery

forever. The princess wasn't meant

for a man like him.

Mechanic

Donnchadh

An hour later, Donnchadh was relieved to float into the dock of the Holo Ocean Space Station. A huge robot came to slot them into a spot, and Donnchadh was grateful that they'd been lucky enough to arrive here. He had to stop Princess Celeste from doing any more damage before he could deliver her.

She was still sleeping in her

bedroom, so he went quickly into his room to grab cuffs. While she slept, he cuffed her to the headboard of her bed. She wouldn't be going anywhere while they were at this space station. She'd proven that she couldn't be trusted. He didn't want to tick her off too much — she'd be the wife of the most powerful man on the planet where Donnchadh was training — but he really hated to think about how much more she could do if she decided to smash the control panel.

He didn't like what he did next,

but he had to do it. He put more sleeping gas near her so that she breathed it in. If he brought someone else onto the ship, he couldn't have her waking up and demanding to get out.

KSM would probably be able to smooth over any problems with local authorities, but they didn't have much of a presence on podunk space stations in the middle of nowhere.

He left her inside of the ship, still asleep behind a closed door, as he went to look for a mechanic to fix the engine.

He went into the station to find one. Most of them were already busy with other customers, except for the most expensive one. Donnchadh winced when he read the services menu, but he didn't have a choice. KSM would cover it, anyway, as a necessary maintenance expense.

The mechanic came with Donnchadh back to his spaceship. He unscrewed the panels that hid the engine and power center from damage.

He whistled a descending note.

"Wow, this one is a doozy."

"Can you fix it?"

"I'm afraid not. Extremely important components of the engine are now damaged. I'd say that you need to replace the entire thing."

"How much would that cost?"

"Believe me, boy, you don't want to know."

He'd be stuck on the space station, sitting and waiting until someone could fix it. How humiliating to fail on his very first mission.

"Thank you, sir."

The mechanic saluted. "I'll charge KSM for the cost of a service call."

Donnchadh nodded before the mechanic went away.

Without power on the ship, Celeste and Donnchadh couldn't possibly stay. Donnchadh had a credit pass for this mission, it was true, but the expenses kept piling up. He needed to stay in a place where he could secure Celeste and stay safe himself while waiting for backup to arrive, after he called KSM to apprise them of the situation.

He needed to move fast, before she woke up. If she was awake, she'd be a wildcat, and he wouldn't be able to control this situation. He had a limited amount of sleeping gas, and he was using up his supply. Somehow, KSM standard provisioning didn't take into account the situation of transporting a Bride who needed to be put to sleep the entire time; obviously, nobody had been as feisty as Princess Celeste before.

The thought made him grin, but he ran quickly through the docks to look for a hotel.

Reception

Donnchadh

He went into the nearest one, which was called Olmito.

"Hello, sir! How can I help you today?"

"I was looking for a room for me and my companion. And, uh," he said, lowering his voice and giving her the stare that some girls loved, "it needs to be soundproof....if you know what I mean." He winked at her. He might not have a lot of experience with women, but he could channel his inner Gairbith. His brother lived to chase women and excitement, and Gairbith was the kind of guy who would show up at a hotel just to rent it for an hour.

"Oh, sir, if you want soundproofing, there's only one suite that we have for that."

"What's that?"

"The honeymoon suite...it's for newly mated couples."

"Sounds perfect," Donnchadh

said. "Here's my credit pass."

He wasn't spending his own money, so he didn't feel too bad about the cost, which was non-trivially high. KSM had given him the credit pass in order to pay for necessary expenses, and after Princess Celeste had totally killed the ship, lodging was the least of their worries.

That reminded him. KSM needed to hear about what was going on. He found a public glow pad in the lobby area of the hotel so that he could check in with Sergeant Park. The glow pad buzzed twice before it asked him, "Name?"

"Donnchadh." The first name was unique enough to identify him.

"One moment, please."

"Donnchadh!" boomed Commander Stark's voice as his image was projected in front of Donnchadh. "How is your first mission going?"

"Not well, sir. She disabled the spaceship."

There was dead silence on the

line for a moment.

"How did she manage that?"

"She pulled out a bunch of live wires inside of a generator." Both men knew that it was a miracle that she was alive at all.

"Did you get it fixed?"

"I re-attached them, but I got a mechanic at this small space station to look at it, and he says that the engine is irreparable."

"I guess that means that we're going to have to shell out a lot of this contract money."

"Yes, sir."

"Fine, fine," Commander Stark said, waving his hand. "The most important part is that you have the girl."

"I do, sir."

"Make sure it stays that way."

"She's likely to attempt to escape, sir."

"Keep her handcuffed to the bed. But no funny business," Commander Stark laughed. "Not that you ever get up to any."

For some reason, Commander

Stark's comment made Donnchadh feel self conscious about his sex life...or lack of it. There were enough tourists who came to Dalat to take pictures and hike around their forest, checking out the unique flora and fauna, that he could find some willing women any night that he felt inclined to find one.

Princess Celeste was not one of the standard tourists. He needed to get her into the honeymoon suite before she woke up.

"Sir, I need to get back. I've dosed

her with sleeping gas, and it should be wearing off now."

"Be careful," Commander Stark told him. "I don't want you to lose your first Bride on your first run by yourself."

"I will be," Donnchadh promised.

"Dismissed." They saluted each other, then Commander Stark was gone. Donnchadh needed to get back to the ship.

Sneaking

Donnchadh

He got back to his ship and realized that he wasn't going to be able to carry a full-grown woman through the docks without being noticed. The ship had huge duffels that were big enough to fit the petite princess into, if her legs were bent. The standard KSM duffels would be sufficient for this task.

She was still asleep when he

came into her bedroom. He bent her legs, then he rolled her so that she was inside of his duffle bag. The cuffs came off of the headboard and were attached around her two wrists.

He was careful as he zipped it up, sure to leave a little bit of room at the end so that she could breathe in there.

Then he was out of his spaceship carrying no extra clothes, just a huge duffel with a young, lovely princess. He swung around the back of the hotel to go into a side door that wasn't the main entrance. He didn't want too many people to see his duffle and its contents.

He finally found the honeymoon suite by following the signs. He immediately unzipped the duffle and brought Princess Celeste out. She was still asleep, for which he was grateful. It made it easier to handcuff her hand to a headboard in here because the headboard had amazing slats which made it easy to attach a pair of handcuffs.

Donnchadh had put his tablet

into a very large pocket, and he was reviewing everything that he saw in the file while he had some downtime. It wasn't incomplete, per se, but it wasn't complete, either. The researchers always did a solid job of researching potential females who might fit the right profile for extraction, and Princess Celeste had all of the right markers. Her scores for beauty, intelligence, kindness, etc. were high enough to ensure that she could be sold anywhere. The man who had Celeste would be very lucky indeed.

* * *

He had to remind himself of that when Celeste woke up. She came awake when she pulled her hand from its position over her head, only to find that it wasn't going to let her move at all.

She screamed.

"Honestly," Donnchadh said. "Don't you think that's getting a bit old?"

She turned towards him. "Sorry, I'm not used to waking up with strange men around. Who are you? Why am I handcuffed to the bed?"

"I'm Donnchadh. You are handcuffed because you already tried to escape once and nearly killed us. I wanted to make sure that you wouldn't have another shot."

"I didn't kill us, though. We ended up at this space station."

"The fact remains that we could have died because of your actions. I'm keeping the handcuffs on you before you do something else reckless and ill-considered."

"It's not my fault that your spaceship doesn't have normal safety features like an emergency pod like the rest of the Intergalactic Federation's ships," she hissed, eyes narrowed. She was a princess to the bone, and she seemed to consider her crazy actions, which nearly got them killed, justified.

He shook his head.

"I'm hungry," she announced.

"Fine. I'll get us something to eat."

"I want écrevisse."

"What is that?"

"Seafood," she said. "I don't know if they have it on this space station, but that's what I want for dinner."

"You're not getting it," Donnchadh told the spoiled princess. "You'll have normal food. That's what I can promise."

"I'll go on a hunger strike if you don't feed me what I want," the princess warned. "How do you think my future husband will react once he finds out that you starved me?"

"I'm not trying to starve you,"

Donnchadh protested. But he could see by the gleam in her eye that she really meant it; she'd try to jeopardize his career if he didn't get her stupid seafood.

He sighed and got to his feet. "I'll see what I can do."

He could feel her eyes on him as he walked out the door, muttering to himself. Even when Saoirse had been a little kid, she'd never been as bad as the haughty and spoiled princess, who managed to issue commands even when she was handcuffed to a bed.

He had almost reached the door when he heard a soft sound behind him. When he turned around, he was horrified to find that Princess Celeste was crying.

"Stars above," he groaned. He'd been trained to withstand a mild amount of torture, but he was no match for a woman's tears, which explained a lot about Saoirse, frankly.

"What's wrong? I'm getting you what you want."

"I don't want to be tied to the

bed," she blubbered. "The cuffs are hurting my wrists."

Donnchadh considered that unlikely, since the cuffs were lined in gel that conformed to the wrists that they were on, but she was kept in the secure honeymoon suite, and he thought that it would be fine to let her stay inside of the bedroom as long as he locked it from the outside.

He took the key and undid her cuffs. She rubbed her wrists after he took the cuffs off, and he saw the red marks on her wrists and felt a pang of guilt. He hadn't meant to hurt her.

"Stay here," he told her. "I'll be back when I can with food."

"Sure," Princess Celeste said. "I'll just rest." She turned over and buried her face in a pillow.

With one last look at her, Donnchadh headed to the door of the bedroom. It had a thumbprint lock on it, and he knew that she couldn't get out. It was good enough to leave her there. He'd have to check the market and then ask around if he couldn't find écrevisse . He had no idea what it even looked like.

Herbs

Celeste

Celeste's heart was pounding as she lay in bed, pretending to be asleep. When she couldn't hear anything coming from the other part of the honeymoon suite, she got up. She was still wearing that stupid dress that she'd worn to the opera what felt like a lifetime ago, but she couldn't help it.

She went to the bathroom, which

had a window with a view overlooking a small garden. She'd been a bit of a tomboy as a young girl, so she was proficient at climbing trees. A balcony wouldn't be any different, right?

She carefully lowered herself over the side, grateful that the honeymoon suite was only on the second floor. Behind her was a tree that would break her fall if she did it correctly.

She dropped straight down and landed right on the tree. She winced from the impact on her tailbone. The drop was going to leave a mark, but she needed to get on her feet. She didn't know how much time it would take Donnchadh to get back. He could've just said that he would find écrevisse to appease her. If he came back in the next few minutes, she'd be in big trouble.

So she got to her feet, sliding from the branch, wincing as she heard the skirt of her dress rip when it snagged on a branch. It couldn't be helped.

She hurried quickly towards the center of the space station. She got a lot of curious looks, but nobody asked why a girl with a torn red dress was walking through the station. They seemed very easy-going.

Finally, she got to a store with the word APOTHECARY in big letters on the window. An apothecary was exactly what she needed right now.

She pushed open the door, hearing the bells chime as she came in. She looked up; they weren't electronic. Strangely, there were actual bells affixed to the door. How odd.

A small man came out of the back.

"Hello, miss," he said, looking at her red dress and then looking at her face. "How can I help you?"

"Hello, sir," she said respectfully, needing his help. "I was just wandering by and wondered if you could help me with some herbs. I'm not from this galaxy, you see, and I'm afraid I'm just not familiar with some of the things that you have here. My mother is an herbalist, and I always try to pick up new herbs for her."

"Oh, you've come to the right place. I always love going on-planet on the weekends and scouting for new herbs. I grow them in the back with grow-lights, you see. It might be more efficient, but the strongest plants are always the ones that grow in real soil."

Celeste nodded, although she knew nothing about agriculture or horticulture. It was a strangely neglected part of her education.

"Now, let's see here," he said. "You want the rare ones, right?"

"Right." Celeste hoped that it wouldn't cost a bundle. She had read the writing on the wall as she came closer to adulthood and her mother had cowered under Oxarex's influence. She had a small bank account where she'd slowly moved any money that she could get her hands on. Oxarex did not approve of Celeste personally spending money, so she'd had to save any money that her mother gave her. Queen Ariane didn't handle any of the kingdom's finances, so Celeste's savings were small, but they were in an account that Oxarex didn't even know existed.

"Okay, then." He pulled out a tray from under the counter. "These are the ones that I keep in real soil. They come at a steep price, but they're the most effective ones I've got. Also the most expensive," he said, winking at Celeste. "But I'll cut you a deal if you want to buy a few."

"That sounds great," Celeste told him. "My mother is fascinated by anesthetics, particularly, and their antidotes." She didn't want to be put under by that stupid sleeping gas again, and she had plans for the kind of anesthetic that could knock Donnchadh out. She would see how he liked it when he was made helpless.

"Well, then, you'll want these two plants," he said, pulling them out. "One will knock you out cold for a surgery, and the other one is used to rouse a patient afterward."

"Sounds perfect," she said. "How much?" She gave him her credit pass, one that she kept inside of a secret compartment in her bra. It was a miracle that she'd had it when she was taken, and she prayed to the stars above that she had enough credits to purchase what she needed.

"Let me just check your credit pass, here."

Celeste held her breath while she waited for the transaction to go through. But then the computer beeped, and he put the herbs into a bag and handed them to her.

"All set, miss. I guess I should have asked you before I charged you for the first two herbs...do you need anything else?" He still had her credit pass in his hand.

"What else do you sell besides herbs?"

"I make my own tinctures and ah...I sell some relaxants. Under the table."

Celeste nodded. She knew what kind of "relaxants" he was talking about. "I don't need any relaxants, but what are tinctures?"

"They are alcoholic extracts of plant or animal matter...only plant matter in my case."

Alcohol would be good.

"I'd love to take some."

"You might want to buy some beer, too. I have my own micro-brewery, and I can honestly tell you that it's the best beer on this station."

Celeste smiled. She didn't know if she could cover it, but she might as well buy from this kind man. He was a good salesperson.

"I'll take a tincture and the beer."

"Sounds perfect." He turned and pulled things out of various cabinets.

"Now, don't mix the herbs that I gave you with the alcohol. You shouldn't drink them together. Drug-alcohol interactions can be very unpredictable, and in the case of the herbs that I gave you, they'd increase the action of the drug a hundredfold. I really don't recommend it."

Celeste said, "I understand the risks." But maybe mixing the herbs with alcohol would be the exactly right thing to do. Donnchadh was quite large, and she wasn't sure how much she should dose him with to knock him out. The sleeping gas was easier in a way, because she wouldn't have to measure it. Escape was not going to be easy; she had to give him enough to make him sleep but not enough for him to die.

The computer beeped again, showing that the transaction had gone through. The apothecary gave her back her credit pass and another bag with the tincture and beer in it, this one a little larger with big rope loops as the handles.

"Thank you, sir."

"My pleasure, miss. You have a nice day, now."

"Thank you."

She walked out of the door, happy and hopeful for the first time since she had been stolen. She had the tools in her hands to get out of this crazy mess.

She thought about just running right now. After all, she was out of her room. But no, that wouldn't work. She knew that the man would come and find her; she was distinctive, after all. Most of the people on this space station were fair-haired, and she stuck out like a sore thumb with her dark hair and torn dress. He'd find her too easily, probably before she could manage to get off of the space station. She had to delay his hunt so that she had time to prepare her escape.

She went back to the hotel, looking at the tree where she'd fallen and bruised her tailbone. She quickly climbed up it with her bags on her arms. It wasn't ideal, but it would have to do. She went the furthest that she could go on the tree branch before jumping to the balcony.

She landed like a small cat, silently dropping onto it. She didn't know if the man had come back yet.

She was happy that she'd figured out a way to get out of her situation. The balance of power had shifted. Before he came back, she needed to mix together everything that she'd gotten. She didn't know how she'd convince him to drink what she'd gotten, but she would. Then she'd get off of this space station and start over somewhere else. She couldn't go back to Elysia while Oxarex lived if her mother didn't understand what had happened...maybe she'd go to a planet with few females. Such planets tended to have very open immigration policies for females. While she wouldn't be able to easily blend in, the governments tended to hold onto what women they could find. She'd be able to get food and lodging on a planet like that, and it would be a good start, even if she was out of credits.

Beer

Donnchadh

Donnchadh paused in front of her door, holding a bag of hot food in one hand. He hadn't been able to find écrevisse anywhere, but he'd succeeded in getting seafood that was native to Cria. He supposed that it would have to do.

He unlocked the door, opening it slowly and cautiously in case Princess Celeste was going to kick and throw things again. He didn't want to hurt her, but he also didn't want to find a vase hurled at his face.

Nothing came flying through the door, so Donnchadh pushed it open a little further. Princess Celeste was seated at the table, drinking a little bit of the local beer. He supposed that she'd taken it out of the mini-bar in the room. She had a bunch of empty bottles on the table.

He felt his heart squeeze when he saw the princess trying to get drunk. Stars, if he had been abducted so that he could be forced to marry an unknown warlord, he'd want to escape in a bottle, too.

He put the bag with the food in it on the table and unpacked their food, placing a steaming plate in front of the princess, careful to maneuver around the bottles. She picked up a disposable fork and ate a mouthful.

"Can I drink with you?"

She rolled her eyes, but she reached for one of the bottles and twisted the cap off before handing it to him.

"Be my guest," she said, as if he were a visitor to her sitting room. She was a princess through and through.

Donnchadh drank some of the beer. It had a strange spicy and bitter flavor to it. The Releons liked their beer, but the beer on this space station was definitely not like any that he'd ever had before.

"Thank you."

"Let me ask you a question. I've been thinking about it while I've been locked up in this bedroom."

Donnchadh felt guilty about

imprisoning her, no matter how temporarily, so he said, "Go for it."

"What would ever possess you to get into this line of work? I don't think that you have the heart for it."

Donnchadh put his beer down for a second, then he picked it up again and started chugging it down.

"This mission is a one-time deal. I didn't want to do it, but my hand was forced."

She looked into his eyes, and he hoped that she could see the truth there. She was curious about his reasons, but he wasn't going to tell a complete stranger about his troubles, even if she was beautiful. He hadn't told Giang about what was going on, and he wasn't about to open up to his temporary captive.

She dropped her eyes and rose gracefully to her feet in a single motion. She walked to the window to look out of it, and he noticed with a frown that her dress was torn.

"Why is your dress torn?" His tongue seemed more clumsy than normal.

Why was the room spinning? He had only had one beer, so he shouldn't feel this fuzzy.

He looked down at his hands. They weren't responding to his commands.

"You drugged me," he slurred, realization dawning as his vision went black.

Finder

Donnchadh

He woke up with a start. The light seemed to stab his eyes, but he had bigger concerns, because Princess Celeste was nowhere to be found in the room. She'd run.

He might have been given this assignment because he had excellent test scores and fit the bill, but he imagined that Ngo Xuong Xi had also noticed Donnchadh's skills at finding things. He'd touched Princess Celeste, and he'd be able to find her.

He closed his eyes to go into a very light trance, breathing in slowly until he could locate her in his mind. She was at the docks. He'd have to hurry, or she might be gone by the time that he got there.

Before he left, he took what was left in his beer bottle. No wonder it had tasted strange. The bitterness must have come from the drugs that she'd tricked him into taking.

As he went downstairs in the

hotel, he hailed a passing levi-car. It would get him to the docks in time for him to catch the princess. Having an unlimited expense account was a lot of fun, especially when KSM wouldn't care about what he charged. The contract with Ngo Xuong Xi had to be crazily lucrative for them to give him an open line of credit.

He walked along the line of ships, feeling Princess Celeste's presence inside of a tourist ship called Cyrena. He went to the guard.

"Hello, sir," he said, slouching to

make himself seem smaller and less threatening.

"Can I help you?" The guards on tourist ships cared about customer service just as much as any other hospitality employee.

"I was wondering if I could take a look around really quickly? I've been thinking about taking a pleasure trip, and I'm not sure which ship I'd like to go on."

"Sure, sir. Feel free to take a look around. Most of the passengers are on-planet at the moment, so you'll find that it's fairly deserted, far more so than during a trip."

"Understood," Donnchadh said. "I just want to take a quick look."

The guard opened the door, and Donnchadh walked in. He would never take a pleasure trip on Cyrena. Their security was abysmal. He walked around and knew that Princess Celeste was in front of him, but he had to find his way around the ship walls, hard when he had never been there before. He went through a seemingly byzantine set of corridors before he finally found the door to the room where she was hiding.

When he opened it, he smelled Princess Celeste's perfume. She was in here. He looked around the room before she flung herself at him, hitting him around the midsection. If she'd been the same size as him, maybe it would have some kind of impact, but he was easily twice her weight. He disentangled himself from her arms and picked her up by the ankles, making her skirt fall downward and reveal her leggings.

"You're coming with me, princess. You can come quietly and easily, walking on your own feet, or you can drink some of your own medicine."

Princess Celeste said something, but it was muffled by her skirts.

"What? I can't hear you."

"Put me on my feet," she shrieked.

"Princess, we are not in Elysia anymore. You don't get to command me."

"I'll walk on my own feet. No need

to drug me. It's calibrated to your weight, and believe me, that wasn't easy. That's why I had to fix so many beer bottles. Stars above, I thought that I'd gotten away. How did you find me?"

"I can find anything that I've ever touched. You promise not to make any trouble?" He didn't know why he was even giving her the courtesy of leaving the ship under her own power. She'd proven that she wasn't particularly trustworthy and she would run at the earliest opportunity.

"I promise," she sighed. "I guess you can find me wherever I go."

"Correct," he affirmed. "It's nearly impossible for you to get away from me." Gairbith had managed it, but he shared Donnchadh's skills.

He linked their arms together before towing her away from Cyrena's engine room. To his surprise, the door to the spacecraft wasn't manned when he came back. He supposed that the guard had gone for a walk around the perimeter or something. He was grateful that he didn't need to explain why he'd gone into the ship alone and was now coming out with a second person.

He pushed her into the levi-car that would take them back to their hotel. Her arms were crossed; she looked out the window, not looking at Donnchadh.

He felt bad about stealing her after she thought that she'd successfully escaped, but he couldn't help what he was doing. He was a tool being used for a job. Did he need to take responsibility for what he did when he was just following orders?

Thief

Donnchadh

When they got back to the hotel, he hurried Princess Celeste through the lobby. It was full of people who had no interest in the two of them, and he quickly got them back to the honeymoon suite. As soon as Donnchadh had brought the princess back to the bedroom, he grabbed the handcuffs that he'd used earlier and attached her to the headboard.

"Hey! I said that I wouldn't try to escape again, especially not after I found out that you can track me wherever I am."

"I'm not going to waste time hunting you down again," Donnchadh told her, his voice as cold as the dark heart of winter. "You'll stay here until I can fix my ship and we can get off of this tiny space station."

"Help!" Celeste screamed, showing spirit that she hadn't shown downstairs in the lobby. "Help me!"

"Hush, princess. There's nobody to hear you."

She thrashed against the handcuffs, knocking the headboard against the wall. No matter how hard she struggled, though, she couldn't break them or the headboard.

Donnchadh frowned. He'd be glad when this was over, when all of the credits were in his account and he'd be able to ensure Saoirse's safety. This mission was horrible. He hoped that he wouldn't be required to become so personally entangled with future extraction targets.

"I'm going to get the engine repaired or replaced. You're going to stay here until that happens. I'm not going to fall for your tricks again. I've got to finish this job. I can't fail."

Princess Celeste didn't say anything as Donnchadh got to his feet and left her there, handcuffed to the bed. He'd be back as soon as he could.

* * *

Several hours later, Donnchadh returned to the room. It had taken many trips to different mechanics, but he'd finally found someone to replace the engine. The spaceship would function well enough to take them back to the base on Dalat; there, he could get the KSM mechanics to do whatever they needed to do. The small space station didn't have that many things, so the best he'd been able to do was a used engine from a damaged spaceship. He sighed. This mission really hadn't gone as planned.

When he saw that the door to the

honeymoon suite was open, he frowned. He had definitely locked it. Princess Celeste might be handcuffed to the bed, but he would never leave the outer door open.

He quietly went to the door and looked through it. He heard a click as the bedroom door's retina lock disengaged. He closed the door behind him, grateful that the hotel maintenance bots kept it in perfect working condition so that it didn't make a sound.

The door to the bedroom was

open now. Had Princess Celeste found someone to break her out of the room? This hotel really wasn't a secure location, but it'd been the best place that he could find.

He swiftly crossed to the door of the bedroom, where he saw a man dressed in pure black at the end of the bed. He was touching Princess Celeste's upper thigh.

"Well, what do we have here? A real pretty lady handcuffed to the bed. You like kinky games during your honeymoon, darling?"

"Get away from me," Princess Celeste snarled. She tried to kick the intruder, but he just laughed and dodged.

"No, I won't be getting away from you. First, you're going to tell me where any credit passes you have are. Second, you're going to get that beautiful dressed ripped from your tender little body while I take what I want."

She began to thrash on the bed in earnest, but she was tied too tightly.

"Maybe I'll do the second thing first. You're a pretty little thing. Your dress obviously shows that you're wealthy, even if it's torn. I noticed you when you were at the apothecary."

Donnchadh realized that Celeste must have gotten the drugs somewhere; he'd deal with her later. Right now, he needed to save her from possibly being forced while she was handcuffed to the bed.

He drew out his laser gun and set it to the highest setting, which could cut diamonds.

"Hands in the air," he said, coming into the bedroom. Princess Celeste's body relaxed, and she stopped moving.

"Who are you?" the intruder said, turning to look at him. "Her heroic husband, all ready to save his lady love?" He must have thought that the conversation would distract Donnchadh, because he lunged for Donnchadh's laser gun.

But Donnchadh had been trained from childhood to fight, armed and unarmed, and he kicked the intruder's knee, shattering his kneecap. The intruder shouted in pain, and Donnchadh aimed for the intruder's thigh on the opposite leg. He wasn't shooting to kill, but he could effectively immobilize the thief until he could get the hotel security to capture the intruder. Donnchadh ignored the shouting thief now that he was neutralized.

He went to Princess Celeste, trembling on the bed.

"Did he hurt you?"

"No."

"Good. Because he wouldn't walk out of here alive if he had." If the intruder had forced her, Donnchadh would be reporting a homicide out of self-defense instead of a simple break-in. The thought of someone hurting her on his watch made his blood boil; he thought that she'd be safe enough in the honeymoon suite, but he had been totally wrong.

He uncuffed her from the bed. "I don't know what you did to attract his attention, but it's clear that it's not safe for you outside of the hotel and even inside of it. I want you to stay right here, okay?"

She nodded, her breath coming in shallow pants. He knew that she was going through a mild panic attack after almost being forced, and he regretted ever cuffing her to the bed. Surely there was a more elegant solution to keep his wayward captive.

He casually hit the intruder, who was writhing in pain on the floor, with the butt of his laser gun, knocking him out cold. When the intruder woke up, he'd have a huge lump on his head, which was the least that he deserved after coming in and trying to rob Princess Celeste.

He dragged the intruder out of the room, not bothering to be gentle. He'd have rug burn, and he deserved it. He pulled the man out of the honeymoon suite and into the corridor. He knew that the hotel security checked the monitors, and sure enough, after only a minute there were hotel guards outside of his room.

"What's going on, sir?"

"This man tried to rob us inside of the honeymoon suite. I have to say that I'm disappointed that he could get in. My lady and I were very upset."

"I'm sorry, sir," the hotel security guard told him. The other one was picking up the unconscious intruder. "We'll report him to the police, and I'll talk to the manager about providing some recompense for the hassle."

Donnchadh shook his head. "It's not my money. I wouldn't say no to having some kind of security bot outside of my door, though. I don't know how he opened the door, since it was retina-locked, and I think that we may need a little more."

"We'll bring a security bot that does body and temperature scans, sir," the helpful guard said. "We only use it for dignitaries, but we may as well use it now. It wouldn't do if the hotel got a reputation for allowing its guests to be robbed, sir."

Donnchadh understood what the guard was getting at. "As long as he's brought to justice, nobody needs to hear about this."

"Good, sir." The guard nodded at Donnchadh and headed after his colleague to take care of the thief.

Untouched

Celeste

When Donnchadh got back into the room, Celeste was still shaking from the close call with the intruder.

"Are you okay?" Donnchadh asked her again. "Is there something I can do? Do you need warm tea or something?"

Celeste shook her head. She was about to say something that was crazy, but she'd say it anyway.

"I want you to hold me."

He stilled. "What?"

"Hold me, please." She could feel tears welling up. "If you hadn't come back when you did..."

Donnchadh's face softened, and he came to the bed to wrap her in his muscular arms. He maneuvered her so that her head was on his chest. Her head went towards his shoulder while she put one hand over his heart, noticing how firm his pectoral muscles were. He felt like a warm rock.

"It's my fault that he even got in. I should've set up a better set of security measures."

"I don't know what he had, but he got past the retina lock on the outside of the door, so it must have been pretty sophisticated. Why would a thief with that kind of equipment come to steal from someone with a torn dress?"

"I think that he wanted more than just your credit passes, Your Highness. He noticed how stunningly beautiful you are and wanted to take a bite out of you, unwilling or not."

"You think that I'm stunningly beautiful? I'm a mess. All my makeup is gone and I've been wearing this same dress for a while now. I'm at my most disgusting at the moment."

He laughed and stroked her hair. "You could never be disgusting, Your Highness."

"Call me Cee, please. We're in bed together. I think that we're beyond the place where you need to address me according to my station."

Donnchadh shifted a little bit.

His hand stopped stroking her hair.

"Don't get out of bed, please."

"I can't..." His breathing was getting a little strange. "You have to be untouched."

"What?"

"You aren't the standard KSM Bride. You're supposed to be untouched upon delivery."

The knowledge was enough for Celeste to raise her head and look Donnchadh directly in the face.

"What? It's a condition of the delivery for me to be a virgin? How would they even know that I haven't had sex?"

"They're very thorough with their research. In the case of virginity, they'd check your medical records. Have you had a doctor's visit in the past few months?"

Celeste thought about it. She went for an annual checkup at the start of every year, but Oxarex had sent her to the doctor only two months ago to get checked for cervical cancer. Cancer was simple to treat if it was detected early enough.

She had no idea why Oxarex thought that she had cervical cancer. But now, knowing that Donnchadh's employers needed to check whether or not she was a virgin, it finally made sense.

"Yes." She laid her head back on his shoulder. "I haven't had much of a chance to see anybody."

His hand went from her hair down her back, settling at her waist. She felt warmth radiating from his hand which spread to her stomach, kindling a small fire in her gut that made her insides liquid. She felt her heart sing at the affectionate intimacy, something that had been missing from her life for far too long.

"I need to get us some dinner. I'll be back soon. Keep the door to the bedroom locked."

She liked the way that his deep voice made his chest rumble when he talked.

"Okay," she sighed, half-asleep from being held like this. It was as good as a lullaby.

He gently eased her off of his

shoulder and wrapped a blanket around her. She opened one eye to see Donnchadh's faced filled with affection.

She yawned. Though she'd been handcuffed to the bed for several hours, she hadn't slept while she strategized and tried to wriggle out of the cuffs.

"Stay safe."

Then Donnchadh was gone, and Celeste fell asleep, warm and cozy in the bed, feeling secure for the first time since she had been stolen.

Dress

Donnchadh

Half an hour later, Donnchadh came back with another bag of food. This time, he only had simple sandwiches, knowing better than to ask Princess Celeste what she wanted. She'd sent him on a fool's errand before so that she could sneak out and go to the apothecary, where the intruder had seen her, to drug him. He really couldn't blame her for trying, though.

She was asleep when he came back to the room, bundled up in the covers. He touched her shoulder and shook her gently.

"Wake up. It's time for dinner."

Her beautiful eyes opened. Donnchadh was trying to get used to her stunning beauty, but it was hard. Every time that he saw her was an echo of the first time. When he'd been holding her in the bed at her request, he'd been as hard as a rock and grateful that the inexperienced princess didn't notice the tell-tale sign of his arousal.

She unwrapped herself from her cocoon of blankets to come sit at their table. She opened the bag with food and took out a sandwich, unwrapping it and taking a bite. After she swallowed, she asked, "What's in the other bag?"

"A present."

"Present?" She took another bite of her sandwich before putting it down. "What kind of present?"

"It's one that I think that you'll

like."

When Donnchadh went out for food, he had also stopped in the boutique near the hotel and bought a dress that he thought might be Cee's size. He wasn't an expert in women's fashion, but he did have a sister, and she sometimes dragged him along to go shopping. He chose a simple ocean blue dress so that it wouldn't look as if she were a wealthy princess, and that would definitely deter any future thieves from coming into their hotel suite.

"It's lovely," Cee said as she pulled it out of the bag. "It's a very nice color. The fabric feels so smooth and soft."

"I'm glad you like it, Cee. I'm hoping that nobody will come after you if you're wearing a simple dress."

"We can certainly hope so." Celeste took another bite of her sandwich before putting it down.

"I'll just go change in the bathroom."

She walked into the bathroom with the dress in one hand.

Donnchadh unwrapped his own sandwich and ate it in 5 bites. He stared hungrily at the remnants of Celeste's sandwich, but he wasn't about to steal food from the princess. It was bad enough that he'd stolen her.

"Donnchadh," he heard her say. "Please come in. I need your help. The zipper is stuck."

Donnchadh rubbed his hands together to get rid of the crumbs, then he walked into the bathroom.

He felt his breath whoosh out of

him as he saw the delicate curve of

her back and an acre of exposed skin.

He'd helped Saoirse with her dresses

when she was small, but the princess

in the bathroom was a far cry from

his baby sister.

Looking at the zipper, he could

see the problem. She had some kind

of lacy ruffle on her lower

undergarment, and the zipper had

stuck.

He pulled the zipper down,

tucked the lacy ruffle in, and zipped

up her dress.

"All done," he said, his voice a little rough. He wasn't an angel, and being in close proximity to Princess Celeste and her beauty was getting harder and harder to handle.

"Thank you," she said, turning around him and smiling. He blinked when he saw the front of the dress. In the store, it seemed innocent and demure, good enough for the princess but not sexy enough to entice strange men into their hotel suite.

Now that it was on her, though, he could see that there was some kind of keyhole opening right at her breasts. He got a good shot of the shadow created by her cleavage every time that she breathed.

He had to turn away at that point.

"You should finish your dinner," he said, trying to get his breathing under control.

"Okay," she said nonchalantly, and he knew that she hadn't noticed how aroused he was. She walked out of the bathroom behind him. He curled up on the bed, facing away from the princess so that she

wouldn't see how the prolonged and

enforced proximity was impacting

him.

Bribe

Donnchadh

He heard the scrape of her chair when she sat down at the table and ate the rest of her sandwich. He heard her crumple the wrapping paper when she was done. She cleared her throat.

"I have a question, Donnchadh."

"Yeah?"

"Why are you doing this? I don't think that you seem like the average kidnapper."

Donnchadh swallowed hard. He could tell her; it was the least he owed to the captive princess. "I'm not. I had to take this contract. My brother, stupid Gairbith, got into debt. A lot of debt. The men to whom he owes the money are trying to collect from me and my sister. They killed my father already."

She gasped. "That's horrible."

"We thought that it was just a stupid levi-car accident, but Gairbith disappeared soon after my father's funeral."

"But you're a finder...can't you find him?"

"Gairbith's a finder, too. He knows what to do in order to escape."

Celeste was quiet for a moment. "What do you need to do in order to escape?"

"You have to be a finder in order to do it, but you just change your pattern in order for me not to be able to find it."

"Change your pattern?"

"Yes. When I touch someone, I

pick up their pattern. I can find it anywhere. It's not easy to change yours, and only a finder would be able to tell the difference between his first pattern and his modified one."

"I see." He hoped that Cee wouldn't try to escape again. He thought that they were really bonding, especially now that he had let his guard down.

"I'm not worried about myself," he told her. "If I only had to worry about myself, entering KSM would've been enough to protect me." The thugs had come in and roughed up Giang, but he doubted that they would kill anybody inside of a KSM base. It would be suicide.

"Who are you worried about? Gairbith?"

Donnchadh snorted. "No. Gairbith can spacewalk for all that I care. No, I'm worried about my baby sister, Saoirse. She is just 18 and about to go to healing training." Donnchadh didn't add that he'd taken an advance against the proceeds of this mission in order to fund Saoirse's training.

"And you think that she's at risk?"

"I know that she's at risk. Mr. Cross is nobody to tangle with, but Gairbith doesn't have a good sense of self-preservation. He lives in the moment, so he rarely thinks of the future or how his actions might impact the rest of his family." He sighed. He might as well tell her about the attack; it wasn't as if she'd report the incident to KSM. "I've already been struck."

"What?"

"They trashed my room at the base. My roommate got a black eye, even though he's a very skilled fighter with some precognition. They caught him asleep, and I think that there were too many of them for him to fight off successfully. They tore apart my room looking for me. The cost of replacing furniture just about wiped me out, and I didn't have a lot to begin with. If I don't pay back the debt, then Saoirse will die."

She was quiet for a moment. "We

can fix that. If money is the only problem, it's not a problem. I can talk my mother into giving you a reward for my return. We can send for your sister and relocate wherever you want. We'll fund it."

"You can't be sure of that, and the debt is an incredible amount. I'd rather take the sure thing."

"So you'd rather kidnap me for KSM than return me to my own kingdom?"

"It's not about my personal preference," he told her, trying to convince himself. "I've got to do this job for Saoirse's sake."

"But if you return me, then my stepfather won't be able to take over the kingdom once my mother dies. Our country is always ruled by a female monarch, but he's probably going to put one of my idiotic stepsisters on the throne. The fate of Elysia is in your hands."

Donnchadh hated feeling helpless.

"Listen, princess, I am just as trapped as you are."

He heard her begin to cry behind him, and he would've rather been beaten by Horus than listen to her sobbing. He wouldn't be manipulated by her tears into doing something for her again, but he felt the urge to fix the problem.

He got to his feet and picked up the princess, ignoring the squeak of surprise that stopped the flow of her tears.

"Come here, princess."

He held her in the same position that they'd been in earlier, when she'd been quivering from the aftermath of the intrusion. She cried into his shoulder, even though he was the one doing all of this to her. Her arm was around his waist. Donnchadh wished that he could help her or turn back, but his hands were tied.

They fell asleep like that, arms wrapped around each other, hearts troubled by what the future held.

Change of Heart

Donnchadh

The next morning, the two of them got out of bed. Princess Celeste seemed resigned to her fate; she'd tried her best to escape, but she couldn't possibly get away from him. She didn't struggle as they walked towards the docks with their gear in tow, and Donnchadh's guilt was almost a physical thing, a weight between his shoulders.

They were both quiet as they entered the ship. The princess went into the bedroom that she'd stayed in before while he launched the ship off of the space station and towards Dalat. They were on course, and the ship would arrive in less than two days, less than one if they flew straight through space. If any Elysians came looking for Princess Celeste, they wouldn't be able to find her. The nav cards had them spiraling through different paths, staying off of the major transit routes.

He understood now why Ngo Xuong Xi had asked for someone with his flight skills; even if they got "lost", he'd be able to get them back on track with just the standard KSM paper maps. He couldn't say the same about even half of his KSM regiment.

The beautiful princess seemed to understand Donnchadh's desire to protect his little sister, and he felt horrible about delivering her to the warlord. He didn't know that much about Ngo Xuong Xi, but he knew that he'd never let the warlord even meet Saoirse, let alone marry her. He'd fallen asleep last night with the princess's tears making his shirt damp while he held her in his arms. How could he possibly give her up?

He'd rejected her offer out of hand last night, but in the morning light, he wasn't so sure. He might have been too hasty.

He went to her bedroom, where she was curled into a little ball. He could see her shoulders shaking as she cried noiselessly. Her spirit was broken, and the thought hurt him like a knife in his windpipe. He sat on the other half of her bed.

He was both a prisoner and her warden. How could he do to her what Mr. Cross seemed intent on doing to him? For all he knew, being married to Ngo Xuong Xi could be a fate worse than death. It seemed strange that he'd asked to extract an Oxitan princess rather than any of the immigrant women who came to Dalat for a better life. If he wanted a wife, the most powerful man on Dalat could certainly have one.

Instead, he'd gone through the trouble to use KSM to take an Oxitan princess as a wife. He knew that Dalat was a former Oxitan colony, before they'd joined the Intergalactic Federation and set Dalat free. Perhaps the scheme to steal a princess and wed her was part of a revenge scheme. The Oxitans had been brutal to Dalat, decimating the population, enslaving them for their own purposes while they looked for resources on the lush planet full of people who were initially welcoming and open-handed. Most of the architecture was influenced by the Oxitan colonial period. It wasn't so long ago that Oxitan had finally given it up; if it hadn't been crucial to their entry into the Intergalactic Federation, they wouldn't have. Dalat was a major prize. There was definitely bad blood between the Yuenanren and the Oxitans. He didn't know much about Ngo Xuong Xi, but it was certainly possible that the rest of Princess Celeste's life could be spent being a whipping boy for Ngo Xuong Xi's anger towards Dalat's vicious and ruthless conquerors. KSM screened every potential customer, but that didn't mean that they would find anger that bubbled beneath the surface for sins committed long ago.

He really couldn't do that to her and look at himself in the mirror every night. There was the barest thread of a chance that Princess Celeste's mother could help him save Saoirse and himself from Mr. Cross, and while he still breathed, he might grasp that tiny thread and hope.

"Princess?"

He saw her wipe her eyes before she turned back to him and sat up. His heart hurt when he saw that her eyes were red, though her perfect princess posture never changed. She always acted as if she were in control of the room.

"How long do I have?" she said, wiping the corner of her eye. "How much longer will my freedom last?"

He sighed. "I don't know. I can't

guarantee your freedom, but I'm not going to deliver you to Ngo Xuong Xi."

"Really?" she said. "Is that a cruel joke?"

"No." He swallowed. "It's not a joke."

"You'd give up Saoirse for my sake?"

"If you can save her."

"We can. My mother might be...well...Oxarex might cause some problems, but I think that we can convince my mother to help your little sister. Once she realizes that Oxarex arranged to have me kidnapped, I hope that she'll listen to me and divorce him. He's not fit to be her consort and never has been."

"I'm going to hope the same thing, Your Highness."

First Orgasm

Celeste

Donnchadh moved as if he'd get off the bed, and Celeste put her hand on his shoulder.

"Hey," she said softly. He turned to face her. She saw the grim set of his mouth and knew that he was thinking of his little sister's life, which might now be forfeit. "We'll fix it, I promise."

She couldn't blame drugged

alcohol or anything but his dark, masculine scent for what she did next. She found herself putting her mouth on his. There was gratitude, sure, because he'd finally decided to set her free. But there was warmth and the seed of love unfolding, too. He'd saved her from himself and the might of KSM at great personal cost, and she had to hope that his sacrifice had been worth it.

He was initially shocked, but then she felt his hands settle around her waist, the fingers meeting for a moment. Then he laced his fingers together in the center of the small of her back and brought her closer to him, so close that she was straddling his lap as they kissed.

He broke their kiss and scattered kisses on her neck, going down to her shoulder before coming back up to bite her ear. Celeste's body had never felt anything like it; she felt like she had a small sun coming to life in the pit of her stomach, its fiery rays radiating throughout her body.

She bit him back, biting his ear

first before kissing him right underneath his jaw. He moaned quietly in his throat, so she took that as encouragement. She nipped him right where his neck met his shoulder. He gave out a muffled yell.

Suddenly, she was flat on her back, Donnchadh on top of her.

"You're going too fast," he told her. "Are you sure you're a virgin?"

"Yes."

"I'm going to check," he told her, dark promise in his eyes. And then he was flipping her over to undo the zipper that he'd helped her with in the hotel bathroom, revealing her to him as he pushed the blue dress off of her shoulders and down her arms. Her undergarments were quickly unfastened and dropped unceremoniously on the ground next to the bed.

She felt Donnchadh pull her up so that she was on her hands and knees. He grabbed the pillows from the top of the bed and put them beneath her stomach. She felt him go behind her, then he parted her legs a little wider.

She gasped as she felt the first touch of his lips to her lower lips.

"So sweet," he told her. "You're so sweet. Stars above, your delicious smell...your creamy taste..."

His tongue plunged inside of her wet opening now, and she felt her muscles clench and then loosen.

"That's right, princess." His hand was coming to her front and rubbing at the front of her pelvis. It felt so good that she pushed her hips towards his hand as his tongue pleasured her between her legs.

His scent filled her nose, spicy and dark. She knew that he wasn't undressed and that he was behind her. She was completely at his mercy; he could do whatever he liked with her.

And she loved the feeling.

Soon, though, the feeling came to take over her entire body. She was shaking in front of him, her hips pressing forward in an unrelenting rhythm as he stimulated her into the first orgasm of her life, the sun inside of her bursting into a myriad of lights while her vision darkened.

When she opened her eyes again, still panting from the incredible orgasm that Donnchadh had given her, she found herself on her back. Donnchadh was beside her now, the pillows replaced where they had been before. He had a hand on her upper thigh, but it was vastly different from when the intruder had done it.

"Did you like it?"

"Like it? I loved it," she said honestly. She turned so that she could kiss him again, tasting just a little bit of her juices on his mouth. "It's your turn now."

"I'm okay," he said. "I don't want to take advantage of you or this situation." He slid off of the bed, but she immediately followed him and turned him around by pulling on his shoulder.

"Listen," she said. "You don't get to just pleasure me and leave. I know what I owe you."

"You don't owe me anything."

Instead of answering, she pulled

at his pants, unbuttoning them. He said nothing as she unzipped his zipper and released his hard erection, shoving his undergarments and pants down to his ankles and then the ground.

"Cee, you shouldn't feel like you have to do this."

"I want to," she said, her jaw set firmly. "I've never done this before, but I've always been a fast learner."

Fast Learner

Celeste

She pushed him back towards the bed until his legs hit the edge, then she pulled his shoulders down so that he was seated in front of her as she got to her knees. Her mouth watered at the sight of his erect cock; it smelled delicious. There was a drop of liquid at the tip, and she aimed to lick it up.

As soon as it touched her tongue,

she felt her entire body quake with an orgasm more intense than the one that he'd given her with his mouth and hand. It felt as if the spaceship hit a meteor. One moment, she was lowering her mouth to the head of his cock. The next, everything around her moved while every muscle in her body clenched.

"What was that?" she whispered when she could even form words again.

"Some Releons have come that induces orgasms. I'm one of them."

"I want more." She lowered her head to his cock, squeezing the base with her hand. Beneath the base of his cock, she touched the soft balls. He put his hands in her hair as she focused on pleasuring him, putting her tongue on his balls, and he went wild, pulling her away from them.

"So intense. Too intense. The pleasure..." he told her.

She licked her way up his cock in a spiral, sweeping up the salty sweat that smelled exactly like Donnchadh did. She was getting a concentrated

dose of whatever he had. She tilted
her head to the side as she licked the
top of his cock, and his hands
tightened in her hair almost to the
point of pain. She didn't know if she
was doing it right. She released his
cock.

"Are you okay?"

"More," he demanded.

She went back to pumping the
base of his cock with her hand while
sucking the top, a little bit of anxiety
in her stomach because she didn't
know what to do. She'd never been

naked in a man's presence before, so she hoped that Donnchadh was enjoying the oral sex just as much as she did.

All of a sudden, his hips swung forward so much that his cock slid to the top of her throat. His hands were very tight in her hair as he groaned. She felt his thighs tense before he thrust forward again. This time, she could feel warm seed spilling from his rod into her throat. She swallowed it down, and her whole body was again launched straight into an incredible orgasm. This time, with a higher dose, it went on and on, her body melting into a puddle of extreme pleasure while his cock surged in her mouth. He seemed to have an endless supply, and she swallowed the orgasmic juice as best she could, though some of it spilled out onto her cheeks.

Then he was done thrusting inside of her mouth. When he pulled her up so that she was on the bed, her body was still shaky from the aftershocks of all those continuous orgasms — or had it been one enormous one?

"Thank you," he said, kissing her nose. "Wonderful."

"I'm glad you liked it."

He arranged their bodies on the bed so that he was directly behind her, an arm over her waist and his hand right below her breasts. He still had his shirt on, but she liked the feeling of the sturdy fabric behind her. His leg hair was tickling her a little bit, but she didn't mind.

She shifted a little bit, backing

up to get closer to him, and he held her a little more tightly. At the base of her back, she could feel that he was still erect.

"You're hard," she said. Her hand went backwards to tug it like she had before, but he caught her hand before she reached him. He kept it in an iron grip.

"Yes."

Touched

Celeste

Her hand was grasped very firmly in his.

"I want more," she protested, wiggling a little so that her butt caressed his rod. He moaned behind her, bucking his hips against her naked body.

"Princess," he said, his voice strained. He took in a deep breath that she could feel against her back because his chest expanded. "Don't push me any further. I would claim you right here, right now. You're not ready for it. You've never been with a man before."

"I want you," she confessed. His hand loosened on hers enough for her to move it. She flipped over so that she was facing him, moving down the bed so that her face was directly in front of his cock. She opened her mouth wide enough so that she could fit his girth inside.

His hand was on the back of her

neck now, guiding her as she slowly loved him. This time, the small orgasm that she got when his precome came out didn't stop her motion; she'd been expecting it. She cupped his balls in one hand as she continued to milk his cock. He writhed in front of her, grunting as he filled her mouth with his warm come, spurt after spurt filling her mouth and inducing her orgasm.

While he was still spilling his seed, he pulled her mouth away from him. She barely had control of her own limbs, and she gazed at him as he pulled her on top of him and parted her thighs, so that they were on either side of his body.

"Do you want this?"

In response, she put a hand on his still-hard rod and guided it inside of her untouched core. She bit her lip at how full he made her feel with just the tip of his cock inside of her.

"Slowly," he cautioned her.

She slid down a little further, feeling herself open up as he went deeper inside of her body. It stretched and burned enough to hurt, but there was a lot of pleasure to be had, too.

Would there be more pleasure if he went deeper? Only one way to find out.

With a hard push, she moved down his cock until it was fully seated inside of her. His eyes rolled back in his head and his hips bucked up, sending her shooting a foot in the air until he came back down again. His hands were on her butt now, rocking her against him in a fast rhythm.

She'd heard that when a woman lost her virginity, it hurt. She admitted that the feeling definitely burned, and she felt stretched to the limit, but there wasn't much pain. And if there was any, the sensation was being overshadowed by the feeling of him moving inside of her.

Now, he was bucking so wildly that she could barely stay on top of him. She found herself pushed onto her back. His hands came to the inside of her thighs until her legs were pushed wide, her outer thighs flat against the bed.

"You are mine now," he vowed. His eyes met hers as he rode her to completion, finally filling her with his seed. It felt warm when she drank it, but it felt like he'd unleashed burning fire inside of her body when he released inside of her. She felt something moving in a flow towards him.

Then he was gone, leaving a gaping emptiness inside of her where his large rod had been. He easily picked her up in his arms and brought them to the shower inside of the ship's bathroom. As they were cleaned, she looked up at him. He was much taller than her, but he bent to kiss her, his mouth much gentler now than it had been before.

When he straightened up, he said, "We'll find a way out of this, I promise. I'll never let Ngo Xuong Xi touch you."

Her hands went to his shoulders to pull him back down for another kiss.

"I trust you." And she knew that

she did. He needed to protect his sister, but he'd try to find a way to protect both of them.

Wires

Donnchadh

The sonic shower turned off when it detected that both of them were clean, but the two of them stood there in the shower stall, still totally naked.

"What's going to happen next?"

Donnchadh let out a long sigh. "I think that we might need your engine room skills."

"What engine room skills? All I

did was break it. You yelled at me for endangering our lives."

"Maybe you should do it again."

She bent her neck so that she could meet his eyes. "Are you serious? What if we drift into space?"

"We'll do it together, at least. But, no, we're near a Selsa space station this time. I think that we'd be able to recover from your engine sabotage again."

She used his shoulders as she joyfully jumped on him. He caught her butt in his big hands as she connected their mouths.

"You won't regret setting me free, I promise. It'll work out. You'll see."

She wiggled until Donnchadh put her back on her feet. He watched her from the shower stall as she ran towards the engine room. He wasn't dead, so he could appreciate the movement of her hips as she hurried away to set them on an irreversible course.

Who was he kidding? From the moment that he'd given Princess Celeste her first orgasm, he'd been on an irreversible course. He wasn't going to condemn her to a future of eternal misery; she'd done nothing to deserve it.

Then the lights went out. He realized that it was ill-considered for her to do it before either of them had gotten dressed. They'd need to use the portable light to put their clothes back on, but it was a small price to pay.

He went to the control panel and steered the ship just a few degrees towards the Selsa station. They'd be there soon.

He went into the main area, where Princess Celeste was standing. She was looking out one of the star ports, watching the universe swallow them. Sabotaging the old engine was risky, but he didn't see any other choices. The black box would record any moves that he made while he was in command of the ship, and the nano-bots would always tell KSM where to find him.

"Let's get dressed," he suggested. "I like looking at you naked, but I'm sure that the dock master of the Selsa ship would be shocked." The Selsans were a very religious but kind group. They would provide a night's lodging for anybody who needed it and called everybody "friend". He knew that they'd help him contact KSM to get somebody to pick up the ship.

He didn't know what would happen to him. After this failed mission, he didn't know if KSM would continue to employ him; he didn't know if he wanted to be sent on other missions like this one. It wasn't as if he could set all the extraction targets free and keep his job. He'd put everything in the balance for this one reckless gamble to set Princess Celeste free, but his heart told him that it was the right thing to do. It had been troubled throughout the mission, but now his heart was finally at ease with their new path.

Money

Donnchadh

Soon, they were docking at the Selsa station. They went straight to the dock master, who was overseeing the movement of cargo in a loud orange vest that said "Dock Master" on the back, and if he was surprised by Donnchadh's disheveled hair, he didn't say anything.

"I'm with KSM," he told him. "I'd like to contact them, because my engine malfunctioned while in flight."

"I have a Holo Comm in my office," the dock master told him. "You and your lady are welcome to use it."

Princess Celeste put a hand on his arm when he opened his mouth to tell him that Cee wasn't really his.

"That would be delightful, sir. Thank you." The dock master bowed to her before showing them to a small office. He shut the door to give them some privacy.

He still had the card to contact

Ngo Xuong Xi, but he wasn't anxious to learn about what his client would say about the botched mission. He wasn't going to give her up, no matter what.

He called Commander Stark instead.

"Who is it?"

"Donnchadh."

The hologram of Commander Stark sprang to life in front of them. An instant later, Commander Stark asked, "What is it, Donnchadh? Are you done with your mission?" Then

Commander Stark saw Princess Celeste.

"Oh. Halfway done."

"No, sir. We've experienced a ship malfunction."

"Another one?"

"Something's wrong with the second engine, sir."

The commander wasn't fooled for a second. "I guess you don't have what it takes to make it in KSM, son."

"I don't," Donnchadh said. He wasn't cold-blooded enough to kidnap and deliver abducted women every day. It wasn't right, and he wouldn't do it.

The commander sighed. "You had such high test scores, too. Ah, well. We'll just sweep this little failure under the rug; it's bad for our reputation. As long as you can find someone to buy out the rest of your contract with KSM, we'll let you go. It's better for both of us."

"Yes, sir," Donnchadh said, hope rising like a phoenix in his chest. If Princess Celeste's mother could buy out the end of his contract, he'd turn away from his life inside of KSM and never look back.

"We'll send someone to recover the ship from the Selsa station that you're calling from. May the stars shine upon you, Donnchadh."

"You, too, sir." He saluted as Commander Stark ended the call.

"So that's it? You'll take me home?"

"If you can get us transport back to Oxitan, yes. It seems that I'm unemployed now, or nearly."

"It's fine," Princess Celeste

reassured him. "My mother can take care of everything." She leaned forward to kiss Donnchadh.

He sat back trying to figure out what he was doing with his life while Celeste talked to her mother via the Holo Comm, which was several times bigger than the standard KSM glow pad that Donnchadh had in his room back on the base on Dalat. He'd thrown everything away for Celeste's sake, which seemed like an all-consuming gesture worthy of a romantic saga. What the stories didn't say was what happened afterward, when the man was left totally at the mercy of the woman he loved.

He nearly covered his ears when Celeste's mother, Queen Ariane, began shouting at the end of Celeste's story about what exactly had happened before the opera.

"Oxarex told me that you had been stolen at the opera, because of their horrible security. I've had our guards sweeping Elysia and later the entirety of Oxitan looking for you without a clue in sight! It makes sense that you were taken off-planet, and we'd sent people out, but we didn't know where to look. I'll take care of Oxarex, ma petite. Don't worry."

Donnchadh saw that Celeste was glad that her mother had taken her side; she must be doubly glad that her mother apparently now was ready to stand up to Oxarex. Donnchadh saw fire in Queen Ariane's eyes, and that gave him hope that they'd find a way to fix everything.

Mating Ceremony

Celeste

TWO MONTHS LATER

"Get out of the bath, Your Highness," her old nanny commanded. "You'll be late to your own wedding."

Celeste reached for her towel to wrap herself up as she stepped out of the tub. "I won't be late, Nanny."

"Girls these days," her nanny

sniffed. "So rude. When I was a young girl, I was always at least an hour early."

"Of course you were, Nanny." Celeste smiled as she walked into her bedroom, drying herself so that she could put on her dress.

It was a beautiful dress with a modest neckline and loose sleeves. The cut of the dress flattered her curvy body, tight at the top and flowing into a billowing skirt at the bottom. It was beautiful, but the veil was even nicer.

Because Donnchadh was from Releon, she'd researched the wedding customs on his planet. She had a white veil made of Releon lace with gold thread on the edges.

When she looked at herself in the full-length mirror, she could barely recognize herself. She was glowing with happiness in a way that she hadn't been able to in a long time. She had the barest amount of makeup on, just a bit of lipstick, a touch of eyeliner, and a tiny bit of shimmer on her eyelids and cheekbones, but she knew that she looked the best that she'd ever had in her entire life.

She got out of her room and went to the palace steps to step into her own levi-car. Now that Oxarex and his horrible daughters had been cast out of the palace, Queen Ariane had taken over the reins again. Celeste could actually afford to use levi-cars now, and they'd take her to the temple where she would vow to love Donnchadh forever. She could hardly wait, though there were butterflies in her stomach.

The levi-car brought her to the temple. She had no father to lean on, so she made her way up the aisle by herself as everyone in the temple turned to watch her make her way up to Donnchadh.

She focused on him, standing tall and strong at the end of the aisle. And then she was finally there, and her hand met his as the priest began the ceremony.

She repeated the words that she'd rehearsed, and Donnchadh said his vows, too. And then the priest proclaimed them one body. Donnchadh kissed her softly, a promise for more in his eyes.

When she turned, she saw that her mother was crying. They walked down the aisle arm in arm as people threw Oxitan flower petals over them. The fragrance filled the whole temple, as if it were one of the famous Oxitan gardens. She felt blessed to feel the love of so many of her subjects.

Then they were out the main doors. Many Elysians, the ones who hadn't gotten personal invitations to attend the ceremony in the chapel, stood by the street. She got into a levi-car with an open top, and Donnchadh came inside after her, taking her small hand in his. The levi-car brought them in a slow circle all around the capital city as people threw flower after flower towards their car, leaving a carpet of flowers behind them. She couldn't stop smiling. Donnchadh never let go of her hand.

Pregnant

Celeste

After they'd fulfilled their wedding

obligations, they went back to their

suite inside of the palace. They'd

leave tomorrow morning for a fun

tour of the galaxy, lasting for a

month. Donnchadh called it the mi

na meala, the month of honey.

As soon as they were inside of

their room with the door shut,

Donnchadh tore her wedding dress

off of her.

"Donnchadh! My wedding dress cost an absolute fortune." Her mother may have finally taken control of the palace finances again, but her old habits died hard.

"You'll never use it again, m'fhíorghrá," he told her. "You're mine until the day that we die."

He was shedding his wedding robes then, and then he was naked in front of her.

He pulled her into his arms as he kissed her deeply. Then he brought them both onto the bed and pulled her leg over his hip.

"Ready to make a child, a shíorghrá?"

She only smiled at him before guiding his hardness inside of her soft core. They stared at each other as they moved in a gentle rocking motion. She was glad that she had chosen this man to be the father of her children, her mate for life. Releons didn't have the concept of divorce, and she was so happy that Donnchadh had chosen to be with her forever.

Her mother had already issued a visa to Saoirse so that she could come to Elysia and be safe inside of their kingdom's borders. Her mother had also paid the tremendous debt that had haunted Donnchadh and bought out the rest of Donnchadh's contract. They were a little bit cash poor at the moment, but another growing season would bring them back to where they needed to be.

Donnchadh didn't know it yet, but another growing season would bring great changes to their lives. Non-financial changes…

Donnchadh's eyes were closed now, and his flame-colored hair was falling over his eyes as he came near completion. Celeste smoothed it back and then bit his ear.

He shouted as he climaxed, spilling himself into her waiting body. She felt warmth gently lap at her and then consume her as he continued to spurt inside of her.

Then he was done, and, as he always did, he withdrew but pulled her body in front of his. The cuddling that came after making love was always tender.

His hand came to her front. He rested it on the soft swell of her stomach.

"Now that we're married, I wonder how long it will take for you to produce the next heir to Elysia's throne. It's your duty, and I'm happy to help you fulfill it." She could hear the smile in his voice, the promise to try as often as possible to conceive an heir.

She twisted in his arms so that she was facing him. She put her hand on his cheek as she kissed him, then she said, "It's fulfilled."

He blinked for a few moments before she watched the realization show on his face, his eyebrows shooting up two inches.

"You're pregnant?"

She brought his hand to her stomach.

"I am."

He kissed her hard, then he moved down to kiss her soft stomach.

She wasn't showing yet, but she'd have a baby bump soon enough.

"I couldn't be happier to build my life together with you, a chuisle mo chroí," he said as he spread his fingers on her stomach. "I'll protect you and the baby with every breath in my body."

She smiled, happiness fizzing inside of her, as she told him, "I know you will."

Birth

Donnchadh

SEVERAL MONTHS LATER

Donnchadh was pacing back and forth outside of Celeste's room inside of the healer's hall. Donnchadh had been a nervous wreck during the late stages of her pregnancy, remembering all too well that childbirth had stolen his mother from him when Saoirse was born.

But Celeste had reassured him by assembling some of the best healers on Oxitan to care for her, and it had helped somewhat.

Now that the day had come, though, he was nervous. Celeste was far calmer than he was. She'd been taught the breathing and pushing exercises necessary for labor, and she was a champion, easily managing her emotions.

He wouldn't be reassured until both Celeste and the baby were fine.

He watched with nervousness as

more doctors went inside of her room after an alarm sounded. Was the alarm bad? He didn't know, and he wasn't going to get in the way of the doctors while Celeste was delivering.

Finally, a nurse came out, blood on her gloves.

"You can see the baby now, sir."

Donnchadh followed the nurse into the room, where the tiniest baby he'd ever seen was curled up in Celeste's arms. She was as serene as a windless sea.

"Meet our little one," she said,

welcoming him.

He looked at the baby. When they'd learned that the baby was female, Celeste had insisted on naming the baby after Donnchadh's departed mother, Órlaith.

"Hold her," Celeste told him. He held out his hands to accept the little bundle of sleepy baby. Her eyes were barely open, and they shut again when he nestled her close to his heart.

He felt like his heart would burst with love for his tiny daughter as he held her for the first time. He smelled the sweet scent of her head and knew that he would protect her from anybody who ever wanted to harm her. She would grow up to be beautiful, wise, and beloved, just like her mother.

Celeste was smiling drowsily at her husband holding her daughter. He leaned down and kissed her nose.

"Thank you."

She smiled at him. "You did half the work."

"Only the fun part," he said,

grinning. "But I'd be willing to do it again." He winked down at her.

"Maybe in a little while," she said, her eyes closing just as the baby's had.

He placed Órlaith back in her mother's arms so that both of them could rest. His mate and child were in this room, and Saoirse would join them soon so that his whole family could be safe on Oxitan. Saoirse would join a training program here at no charge. When he'd spoken to her on the Holo Comm, she'd been excited to see a new planet.

Gairbith was still gone, but he didn't know if he wanted to see his brother again after the mess that he'd made. He supposed that Órlaith would grow up without ever knowing her uncle; it was probably better that way.

He stroked his mate's cheek as he watched her sleep. He knew that the stars had shone on him to give him the blessing of such a wonderful mate and child.

THE END